ONCE UPON A MEMORY

By

virginia rasmussen

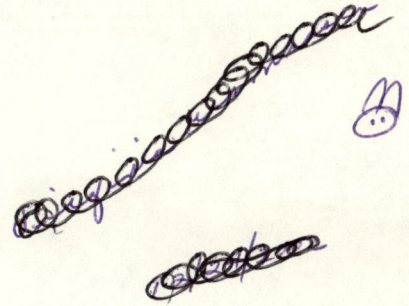

This book is a work of fiction. Places, events, and situations in this story are purely fictional. Any resemblance to actual persons, living or dead, is coincidental.

ISBN: 1-4033-6477-X (e-book)
ISBN: 1-4033-6478-8 (Paperback)

This book is printed on acid free paper.

1stBooks - rev. 10/15/02

Dedication

To my family and friends:

> Kin-Ship and Friend-Ship
> Sail side by side
> Gathering memories
> On the rising tide
>
> Embrace them dearly
> And they'll never depart
> For a memory stays anchored
> On the strings of your heart
>
> Peaceful sailing,

TABLE OF CONTENTS

STORY   PAGE

SAMUEL'S KINGDOM 1
"YOU GOTTA PLAY THE MUSIC LOUD" 88
THE THREE OF HEARTS 111
JUST A SHORT NOTE…... 184

SAMUEL'S KINGDOM

PROLOGUE

Once upon a time there was a small boy named Samuel. Now Samuel had only been in the world a few short years, but in that brief span of time he had been surrounded by enough love, laughter, and joy to last him for a lifetime. But wasn't a lifetime supposed to be forever? Who had stolen those happy sounds? Where had they gone?

Samuel looked under his blankets. There was nothing there. Maybe his closet. Closets could hold an awful lot of stuff. Just maybe the sounds were waiting for a little boy to open the door and let them out. With excited anticipation Samuel gave a quick turn to the shiny round knob on the narrow door. But the only sound that came from the closet was the small creaking noise as the door opened and then again when it closed. "Are you there?" he had whispered. But silence had surrounded him. The toy box! That must be it. With his tiny legs carrying him quickly to the far corner of his room, he couldn't believe he hadn't thought of it sooner. Of course that must be where those missing sounds had gone. They just had to be in there waiting for him to discover them.

Samuel thought about all the many times he had lifted the lid with the funny clown painted on it and could even now almost hear those excited voices next to his side as he rediscovered daily all the hidden treasures that were waiting for him and his eager child's grasp. "Well, look who's hiding in here," someone beside him would say. As the fluffy golden teddy bear with the short red jacket was squeezed, the familiar soft lullaby came from deep inside his favorite companion and filled the surrounding air. Samuel would then take the bear into his own hugging arms and press it next to his "Pooba" pajamas, never releasing his hold until he awoke in the early light of a brand new day.

As Samuel lifted the lid today, he closed his eyes waiting for those happy sounds to surround him once again. But it was not to be. There was only silence. Oh, the bear was there, but he was quiet, too, and he looked so sad to Samuel. Perhaps he was looking for the same things Samuel was, but he couldn't find them anywhere either.

"What are we going to do, Pooba? I think we've really lost them forever. Oh, I can hold you tightly in my arms, like this, and that will help you, but I can't seem to find those strong arms that always held me. Remember how those two great big arms would hold us both and rock us side to side before they would lay us down on the bed? Then the other smaller, softer hands would pull the blankets over us and tell us to 'dream sweet dreams and hold each other to your hearts.' And then we would 'God Bless' everyone we loved so much and after we got that part done we would start blessing all our toys and even the pictures on the walls and the curtains on the windows…just so we could stay up a little longer. Remember those happy sounds we would hear then as our list kept getting longer and longer?

Finally, though, after we had pretty much covered everything and everybody in our own very special, wonderful world, we would be interrupted by that deep, clear voice saying, 'Well, excuse me, little ones, but if I can get a word or two in here for a minute, I was just thinking that maybe, just maybe, you should let some of your other young friends do some of those blessings or I have a feeling they're going to have to go right to sleep when they get into their beds tonight and you certainly wouldn't want that to happen, would you?'

"Remember how we'd look at each other then? It was a pretty hard decision for ones as young as we were. But we seemed to be getting the idea, every once in a while, that there would soon be a lot of times when we'd be asked to make choices, so maybe this was as good a place as any to start. Since we were such close friends, and others don't really seem to hear your voice as clearly as I do, I knew you wouldn't care if I spoke for both of us, Pooba, so I agreed with the deep voice, because I had a feeling that a lot of those friends that were being mentioned, must have given us a good part of their lists nearly every night the way we seemed to be able to go on and on."

The days just weren't the same anymore for Samuel and Pooba. There was still love all around them, they knew that because they could feel it, but it just didn't have that bubbly feeling that it used to have. And instead of all the joyous laughter that had filled the rooms that made up their world, there seemed to be only hushed echoes of days past trying to escape through the thick walls that surrounded them each day. And lately it seemed as if even the memory of those echoes was changing with each new morning sunrise. It was getting harder and harder to remember what they had sounded like and the two young friends wondered if they would even recognize the old sounds if they heard them. It seemed to Samuel and Pooba that there was a quiet sadness now weeping from deep inside those once happy walls.

The strong arms that had once lifted Samuel high into the air so many times in those other days were nowhere to be found and the softer, smaller arms seemed to have lost even their gentle strength now. And yet, there were scattered times when those same arms took on a super strength as they folded around Samuel, and he felt as if he were being locked forever in their crushing hold. It was in those moments that the sounds of sadness were the deepest. If only he could understand why everything had changed.

SAMUEL'S KINGDOM

"Mother, Mother, where are you? Mother? Come quick. I think I have enough. Mother?"

It always took KayLee a few seconds to acknowledge that she was the one being spoken to when she heard the word "Mother". Not that she didn't recognize the excitement-filled voice of her six-year-old son, knew it more readily than any other sound in the world, it was just that he had only recently begun calling her "Mother". The more grown-up endearment had now replaced the second word her young son had learned those several years ago ("Daddy" had taken honors as the first word uttered) in a newly discovered talent known as talking. The time had arrived when "Mommy" appeared to be a word used only by "little" boys, or at least that was the information KayLee had received from her now "adult" child of six.

What a wonderful discovery the spoken word had been those few short years ago. Overnight, Samuel had become an official member of a world filled with delightful sounds and magical words. From that day forward, the bungalow that stood at the end of Pinewood Lane would never be quite the same.

The only thing he had to do, Samuel soon became aware, was repeat the sounds he heard coming from the gentle, but pleading voices that were ever by his side. He would move his tiny mouth and, as if touched by magic, he would hear noises come to the surface and disperse throughout the surrounding air. Those enchanting vibrations, at each occasional utterance, had taken Samuel by complete surprise, even startling him at times. But it wasn't long before his toddler's

5

mind had become so filled to overflowing with the knowledge that he had found a very special, hidden talent that he abruptly made the enthusiastic decision to share it with a most accepting audience.

As thrilling as this newfound talent was to the young child, these strange new sounds held even more delight and surprise for the two familiar figures that were always so near to him. With each spontaneous word he uttered, Samuel would feel arms suddenly encircle him. A strange new excitement sent tingling vibrations from the soft scarlet wisps on his head to the ticklish pink tips of his toes, and the loving melodies of laughter were everywhere.

Laughter. What a wonderful song *that* was. Samuel wanted to hear it over and over again. It was the music that turned a little boy's thrilling new world into a kingdom of magical delight. It seemed to be coming from every direction he turned. It echoed from above. It seemed to come from his every side and then as if he were a magnet, it all came back close to him, flowing and washing over him until he felt immersed in safety, comfort, and love.

The encores were never-ending. And, as if that were not enough, with each new sound and word, the applauding ovations reverberated throughout the space that enveloped him. It was as if he were sitting on a golden throne, being honored by all who came before him. He was the master of his very own kingdom.

—

The change from the premier title "Mommy" to the newly addressed "Mother" had begun only a short week ago. KayLee had taken Samuel to the movie theater located just two blocks from their home. The well-preserved historical movie house, whose white brick exterior had been allowed to age naturally to its present yellowed hue, had a semicircular ticket window outside the entrance, where long lines of local residents, their young ones beside them, could be seen every Saturday afternoon waiting to purchase tickets for the special showing of a Walt Disney classic.

The antiquated theater was located next door to Lloyd's Food Market (whose yearly gift calendar twenty-some years ago had a printing error that mistakenly titled it "Lloyd's *Foot* Market." This error, which would have caused many a merchant to cancel the free holiday give-a-way, instead had introduced the villagers of Morristown to a side of Theodore Lloyd that, until then, no one had known existed.

Humor and cleverness had never been audible or visible attributes of the passive storekeeper. While always portraying dignity in his daily service, this added characteristic to the local merchant's personality had brought about a change in the village's shopping atmosphere and to the shoppers themselves. Where there had usually been looks of sober nonchalance on the faces of the daily customers, smiles were now the routine expression as patrons walked up and down the aisles picking up the needed loaf of bread, the staple quart of milk, or when retrieving the Saturday special, a ring of homemade "German sausage: Made the way your grandma used to make it."

While his fellow villagers had always respected Mr. Lloyd, he was now almost revered. Laughing at one's problems and finding the means to overcome them, had its rewards. Mr. Lloyd had found a way to add some levity to an oftentimes-tedious task…grocery shopping. People responded by returning again and again to Lloyd's Market just to see what Theodore Lloyd would think up next. The now familiar story was told over and over by local inhabitants to all new arrivals the minute a moving truck made its appearance in one of the modest, tree-shaded neighborhoods. The sharing of the incident gave the newcomers an immediate bond with the townspeople, allowing them to feel as if they were already integral parts of the close-knit community.

The tale had unfolded the week before Christmas those twenty-some years ago. On the first day the infamous yearly calendars were to be given out at the local grocery, there appeared in the front display window, a large plaster-of-Paris foot, gaily decorated with colored lights. A sign had been placed next to it that read, "Welcome to Lloyd's Foot Market. If you have never 'set foot' in our store, make it your New Year's resolution to 'step in' and start the year out right. You'll 'get a kick' out of all our low prices and a free calendar 'to boot.'"

(The sign, although sun-faded and rippled with age, and the foot, with a few toes looking slightly worse for wear as time goes by, are yet to this day in the store window and the misnomer has now made the calendar a much sought-after collector's item.)

—

As KayLee and Samuel approached the village entertainment center, KayLee's eyes were drawn to the colored poster at the front of the building. The movie

8

placard, displayed in the glass-enclosed case at the entrance to the aged theater, advertised the present week's attraction, the heart-warming story of Bambi. KayLee had often thought of the lessons of love and friendship that could be derived from what she and the world had always considered a very special story. She was excited for her son to be introduced to the enchantment of this heartfelt tale.

When her life and that of her family had changed so drastically four years ago, KayLee, at that most trying of times, had recalled for some incomprehensible reason the childhood memories she had held of the sadness as well as the heavy train of responsibility that had come along for Bambi. The master of fantasy creations had brought to the motion picture screen this tender story of an innocent member of the animal kingdom. The lessons set forth in this delightful biography had brought to KayLee's sense of realization that days such as those that Bambi had to face can also be very much a part of human lives. She knew that the day could arrive for each of us when we might have to come face-to-face with problems or circumstances that would be both unfamiliar and frightening.

This classic tale, even though it had its sad moments, was beautifully told. Its delightful characters left lasting impressions with all who met them. KayLee wanted to be at her son's side as he watched the story unfold so that she could be a part of his youthful reactions and hear his childhood responses.

The story did have a happy ending and this was important to KayLee, when in real-life she knew from her own experiences, that this was not always true.

But, nevertheless, she was not prepared for the reaction Samuel presented to her as they had left the theater that late afternoon just one week ago.

As the movie concluded and they got out of their cushioned seats to walk up the slanted aisle of the now softly-lighted theater, KayLee felt Samuel's small hand touch her own. As they proceeded to exit through the open door out into the blinding sunlight, she felt a clenching squeeze on her hand. Looking down at the joined hands while waiting for her eyes to adjust to the new brightness of the outdoors, KayLee blinked several times. As her vision equalized, she gasped out loud as she looked at her son's face and saw the frightened, near-panicked expression that had settled there. His eyes were moving from side to side and tears were spilling over his freckle-covered cheeks with each darting movement.

With her heart lurching wildly inside her chest, a rush of panic struck its resounding chord; KayLee felt its startling vibrations throughout her entire body. Quickly leaning down to her son, without releasing the hold of their hands, she asked in what she hoped was a calm voice while feeling anything but calm, "Samuel, sweetheart, what is it? Are you sick? What's wrong? Tell mommy what's wrong."

The tear-filled blue eyes that looked up at her were so wide with fear that KayLee was certain her heart would burst from her chest. She felt her own tears break free as they spilled out onto her face.

Her son's words came slowly and hesitantly at first, but then came rushing out as the dam of tears pushed aside all barriers and gushed to overflowing. "I...I...love you, Mother. Please...please don't ever lea...leave me like...like Bambi's mother left...him. I...I don't want y...you to go...go away. I can't take care of myself. And I don't have a bird or...or a Thumper or even a Flow...Flower to take care of me. And most of all, I don't have a fa...father to tell me to be brave. I'm not even big...big enough to take...to take care of myself, how can...how can I take care of...of others?"

Between each word that Samuel spoke, KayLee heard the deep, spasmodic sobs of a lost, fearful child while at the same time her own loss and fears surfaced at the all too familiar reaction. Dear God, what had she done? She had thought that the happy events of the movie would perhaps wipe out, at least temporarily, the trying times of the past few years, but her son's response had KayLee reeling. She was finding it difficult to think clearly.

Was it possible that the two-year-old child had comprehended more of what was happening those four years ago than the mother had realized? The possibility that he, too, at that time had felt the same clawing emptiness, the same haunting silence that had surrounded her, was making her feel weak and heartsick. In her time of need for comfort and support, had she failed to offer the same degree of condolence to her precious infant child? Could his youthful mind have known and felt the change that had been thrust so suddenly into their comfortably secure family life? Perhaps in her naiveté, in her overwhelming sorrow and prevailing inexperience in dealing with loss, she had unwittingly neglected to give credence to a child's intuitive feelings.

Thoughts juggled about in her mind as she chastised herself for not seeing beyond her own shadow of grief. An article she had read recently in one of her psychology magazines flashed briefly in front of her mental vision. There was the establishing belief, the study had proclaimed, that all things in life are not learned. Many of the feelings and reactions we portray are instilled in us at birth.

Yes, she had lost her husband. That was undeniable. One minute he had been standing at the door hugging and kissing his loving family, lifting his dapple-cheeked son high into the air while listening to the sounds of delight as they bubbled over, spreading far and wide. And then only minutes later he was gone. Gone. Never to return. The only reminder of what had taken him...black marks on a rain-slick highway, shards of broken glass scattered around the heap of crumpled metal.

But this little person, who was now clinging to her so tightly she felt as if they were no longer two separate people but joined as one, had also lost someone that day four years ago. He had lost one of the branches of the tree that had given him life. KayLee had occasionally over the past few years tried to explain to her child why he didn't have a father. Why their family was different from his playmates' families. But she found it difficult to pursue the explanation in length, not only because it hurt her so deeply to talk about it, but also because she was afraid of further confusing her young son. Whenever she started to talk about what had happened, her emotions surfaced, and she was unable to hold back her tears. Hoping to spare him the suffering that she had to bear, she chose silence over sharing. When the door had closed on that last day of being a complete family, joy and laughter had also been shut out; she hadn't been able to let them back in completely ever since.

—

KayLee was certain she was going to be physically ill, could feel the churning deep inside her body, but she knew that this moment could possibly form a mold that her child would carry with him throughout his entire lifetime. She needed to reach for a strength she had been holding back all these years. There was someone whose needs were even more desperate than her own and she found herself taking a deep breath, while praying for the right words to form in her mind.

Gently releasing the vice grip hold her son had on her, KayLee put her hands on Samuel's trembling, fragile shoulders, setting him back just slightly from her so she could look directly into his tear-rimmed eyes. KayLee blinked several times to clear her own rippling vision. Then in a soft, calming tone she spoke with such overpowering love and emotion aimed directly to the center of her dear son's heart that it seemed they were the only two people in the world. She was totally unaware that the same theater patrons who had shared the inspirational fairy tale with her and her child, had now become a participating audience to Samuel's fears. For instead of parting to go their separate ways as the sunlight brightened their surroundings, they had stopped their leave and remained near the exit area of the theater.

Staying within the realm of the unfolding scene, but also maintaining a respectful distance from the personal drama, the entranced onlookers were reduced to facsimiles of statues. Not moving. Breathless. The realization that they were witnessing, in part, a sequel, albeit the human version, to the movie they had all just seen, prevented them from walking away. Strangely, they had all become so enthralled with this true life replay that they had not even given thought to the fact that they might be intruding in one of life's most private moments.

In precise unison they moved their heads to settle their vision first on Samuel then on KayLee. Perhaps, unknowingly, they were waiting for KayLee to provide them with an answer to something they might have to face themselves some day. Instead of the normal discussion chatter that always seemed to take place after the viewing of a movie, the theater's bordering audience held only silence except for the sobbing of one deeply troubled, freckle-faced little boy.

Taking a deep, steadying breath, KayLee applied what she hoped would be the salve that would heal the wounds now afflicting her vulnerable young son.

"Samuel, my precious, dear child," she began, "you must not fill your heart and mind with thoughts of these things. You must enjoy every day and look for all the happiness that surrounds each of us whenever we awake to a brand new morning. I would never choose to leave you. Please always keep that in your thoughts. You are the most important part of my life and we will live and love each other and all that gathers around us for as long as we are here. No one looks for sadness or wants to feel afraid. But when our days bring on some of these unwanted and unknown times, we need to look further ahead for the sunnier days that we know will be coming soon. And they will come. It's the pattern that life follows."

Leaning forward she placed a tender kiss over the tears that were resting on each freckled cheek. With the gentle caress of her hand she then brushed aside the tears that had found anchor beneath the flooded blue eyes, eyes that appeared capable of holding an ocean of salty liquid. Swallowing an extra dose of courage that she seemed to be pulling from thin air, KayLee went on.

"I know this is a lot for a little boy like you to understand right now, Samuel, but you must trust in yourself, in me, and those near you, that no matter what clouds we see, they can still be pretty clouds. I love you, Samuel. I will be your mother beyond all time, just as you will be my son forever, plus forever."

Samuel continued to look into his mother's eyes for a brief moment and then stretching out his arms, wrapped them around KayLee's neck, hugging her with a strength that comes unbidden as it joins the knowledge of a new found faith. "I love you, Mother," he said in a voice that was filled with welcomed relief, "and I always will, too. Just the way you love me. And I promise to always remember that…even when it's a cloudy day. But, just so you know, I do like the sunny ones better."

And then just as KayLee reached deep into her resources for a shadow of a smile, which proved difficult through her tautly stretched emotions, her innocent child found words that erased the darkened edges that had bordered all their natural senses only moments ago. Words that brought about the brightness of a full smile to her heart and to the hearts and faces of the gathered audience, who joined her and nodded assuredly through their own masks of tears.

"You know something, Mother," Samuel said with a note of surprised delight attached to his words, "when you were saying all those important things, you sounded just like Thumper!" And then as a timid smile scattered the myriad freckles on his elfish face, the now comforted child concluded, "That was really a good movie, wasn't it! Maybe we should see it again sometime."

As the child reached for his mother's hand, the two of them stood up once again to walk hand in hand back to their home near the edge of the woods. The now dispersing audience also went on its way knowing, with comforting assurance, that they had witnessed a real life drama that was even more touching and lasting than the one they had just seen portrayed on the movie screen. Nature and its wilderness tales were memorable, but human nature held even more heart-warming and indelible memories.

—

Samuel's excitement-filled voice, erupting with even more enthusiasm as he neared the front door of the white bungalow, pierced KayLee's reverie, and she realized she had been temporarily shut away from the present. Setting the hot cookie sheet briskly down on the top of the stove, giving it an extra shake in order to further flatten the chocolate chipped treats, KayLee ran quickly through the kitchen to the entry way. She pushed open the summer screen door just as her son was opening it from the opposite side. Both mother and son nearly toppled to the sidewalk, but KayLee reached out to grab her son's waving arm and steadied both of them with her free hand.

As mother and son came to a standstill, KayLee heard a clinking sound and glanced downward to see a myriad of silver and copper coins bouncing randomly over the sidewalk. The mother's face lit up with a smile as the delighted voice of her son filled the air.

"Look at all of them, Mother. There must be a million. Help me count again, okay? I think I have enough. I really think I do."

Before he could even complete the sentence, Samuel had nearly all of the wayward coins collected and returned to the small, but bulging, drawstring bag he had been tightly holding in his right hand. The child's diminutive chest seemed to be rising and falling so simultaneously it was difficult to decipher if it was moving in or out. With each breath Samuel took, he tried to release the news that was bursting to be shared. There seemed to be no spaces between the words, just one long racing line.

"Mr.Lloydhelpedmecounteverythingatthestoreandt henIcountedthemalltwomoretimesonmywayhome." Pausing to take a much needed breath, he then added at a somewhat slower pace but one that was still laced with overflowing enthusiasm, "I'll get the rest from my jar and then we'll count one more time just to make sure, okay?"

Clutching tightly the bag of coins in his hand, not wanting to release the hold on his precious treasure for even a second, Samuel ran past the kitchen, racing

17

down the short hallway to his room He returned before KayLee even had time to see if the cookies she had so abruptly set aside were now hardened and stuck to the pan. Cookies could wait. If they were sticking and couldn't be removed without breaking up into crumbs, she and her son would celebrate the joyous occasion that was soon to take place by making ice cream sundaes topped with crushed chocolate chip cookies. Which sounded like a good reason not to even chance removing them until much later anyway.

Watching as Samuel pulled a chair out from its place at the kitchen table and pushed it aside so that he could stand closer to the table, (this was definitely not a sit-down situation), KayLee observed the unfolding scene from her position near the stove counter, feeling the waves of static that were being discharged by one energized little boy.

Dumping onto the table the contents of the peanut butter jar that had just been retrieved from its hiding spot in his closet, Samuel stared in excited anticipation as the coins and folded paper treasures spilled out across the shiny wooden surface of the round oak table. After reaching out to steady the few wayward coins that were threatening to go over the table's edge, Samuel swept his arms out over the entire tabletop to gather with his trembling, eager hands his expanded bounty and brought it to a heap right next to where he was standing. Then as if a bugle had sounded to call him to attention, Samuel suddenly straightened his whole body as if he were a soldier on guard. Taking a deep, steadying breath, he rubbed his hands together several times after which he stretched out his arms as if in preparation for a most challenging task.

Feeling both excited and simultaneously cautious, the child glanced up at his mother who mirrored the exact emotions. But then KayLee smiled and raising her eyebrows while nodding her head, gave Samuel the courage he needed to review the total one more time. It just had to be enough.

Picking up each coin and making piles in determined amounts, he proceeded to stack the folded paper bills in groups of five, until at last he was ready to go for the final total. As his small shaky finger pointed to each pile that stretched across the smooth surface of the table, Samuel's smile became wider and wider, nearly taking over his entire face, until he came to the last heaping stack of coins and then the smile disappeared. His face paled and his eyes widened as he quickly pointed to each set of silver, copper, and paper one more time, all the while shaking his head in disbelief.

Observing the situation from her position at the stove, KayLee watched as her son's face changed from overwhelming happiness to agonizing distress. She felt her own expression drop its fixed, tight creases of anticipated joy as they formed the loose, slacking folds of dread. It couldn't be. KayLee knew that the total should come out exactly right. She had been keeping close tabs on the precise earnings Samuel would need for his purchase, and had even figured out the targeted day that amount would be reached.

Moving quickly around the end of the counter, KayLee came to stand by her son's side. As she moved the chair farther away from the table so she might stand closer to him, she looked down at the chair's legs to make sure they didn't bump into her son's foot. As she did so, she noticed there was something lying next to the front chair leg. Reaching down, she picked up a narrowly folded piece of green paper that had escaped undetected from the mass coming-out event of just minutes ago.

Glancing toward her son, who now had fresh tears dropping onto his red and white striped t-shirt, KayLee smiled and held out her hand, revealing the most important piece of the treasure. The one that completed the total. The look on her child's face was one she was sure she would remember for a lifetime. Relief, joy, gratitude. Every synonym for happiness there could be was written across the freckle-spattered face of the little boy who owned her heart.

"Oh, Momm…ah, Mother," (even while in a state of distraught confusion over his monetary problem, he was still able to catch himself and retrieve the new title he had chosen for his parent), "I just knew it was enough, but…but when I counted everything on the table and it wasn't there… I…oh, thank you, Mother, thank you."

The last part of the sentence that Samuel spoke was muffled as he came close to his mother, hugging her as she leaned down to hold him next to her cookie-scented blouse. She heard him sniffling several times and had a brief thought that perhaps he was again crying, a delayed reaction to the disappointment he had encountered just seconds ago.

"You smell good, Mother, really good. What is…?" Samuel left the question dangling as he pulled back, sniffing a few more times while moving his head side to side to look around the room trying to discover where else the delicious aroma might be coming from.

His eyes lit up as he looked toward the stove at the now cooling cookie sheet and its patterned rows of chocolate chip treats waiting to be pounced upon by the eager hands of one small boy. The aroma had completely escaped his normally alert sense of smell as every part of him had concentrated on the mission at hand.

The excitement of his anticipated fortune had temporarily closed off all his surroundings except for the contents of the small bag he had been holding tightly clenched in his hand and for the full peanut butter jar that he had retrieved from the floor at the back of his closet (removed carefully from its secret hiding place in the sleeve of an old red flannel shirt, a shirt he had found one day on a hook in his mother's closet.)

—

The shirt. There was something about that shirt, something special that had given the child a warm comfortable feeling whenever he touched it. He often thought about the day he had found it and asked his mother if he might use it to hide his jar in the big sleeves. She hadn't answered him right away but instead had gotten such a sad look on her face, that Samuel thought perhaps he should not have asked for it. For some reason, it also seemed very special to his mother.

After a few moments of puzzled silence, Samuel had watched as his mother turned her head aside and with one hand had wiped the corners of her eyes. Then turning back toward to the closet, his mother reached into the closet and removed the shirt from the thick, black hook. Holding it briefly without moving she then softly brushed her fingers over the front of it, letting her hand rest on the pocket flap. Then with a slow, sad smile crossing her face, she had handed the shirt to Samuel. He remembered she had started to say something like, "Yes, Samuel, you may have the shirt. I know it would make him feel very hap..." and then she had stopped and started a new sentence. She had gone on then to say that she thought the shirt was just the thing Samuel needed to hold something that was very special to him.

It was strange, but every time he would pick up the shirt to remove the jar from its sleeve so he could add more of his earnings, a wave of comforting, protective warmth seemed to flow over his entire body. Funny how a shirt could seem to be filled with magic. Samuel's young mind had decided that perhaps that was why his mother liked it so much, too. It must have made her feel the same way. A magic shirt. He smiled to himself each time he took it from its hiding place. He would picture in his mind a vision of the magician who had waved his wand over the plain red cloth turning it into something so mysterious. And then he would think how lucky he was that this special shirt had found its way into his house.

———

"Well, Samuel," KayLee informed her inquisitive son, "I see that you have just discovered the cookies I've been making to celebrate this exciting day. Should we sit down and have a treat or..." the boy's mother hesitated only briefly before adding brightly, "did you have something else we should maybe do first?" Samuel stood rubbing his hands briskly together while his small body moved about as if propelled by springs. Kaylee smiled gently, knowing that not even a dozen cookies would keep her child from being at Shultz's Hardware Store the minute Mr. Shultz inserted the key that would signal the start of a new shopping day.

Looking over her shoulder at the sunflower-shaped clock that hung on the wall above the kitchen sink, KayLee saw that it was five minutes before door-opening time. In forty-five years Mr. Shultz had never been late in opening his store. It was said about town that Everett Shultz had told his wife, Abigail, who over the years had presented him with nine sons and two daughters, that if she felt the time was drawing near for the arrival of their newest addition to the family, she'd better have it here before 9:00 a.m. ...the starting time of a new business day. And being one not to cause any problems, Abigail Shultz was delivered of all eleven children during the wee hours of the morning, thereby allowing Everett to open the store right on schedule!

The townspeople all knew this was just one of the many tales old Everett liked to tell around. A more dedicated husband and father could not be found in all of Morristown and perhaps it was just a deep consideration of respect and love for her husband that came though instinctively on Mrs. Shultz's behalf that the births of all their children had come at such a precise and timely hour.

—

"They smell soooo good, Mother," Samuel offered. And even though he could hardly wait to eat them, there was an inkling toward hesitancy in his voice, "but I…well, what if…what if some other little boy gets there before I do? I think…well, I really think I should be at the store the minute Mr. Shultz opens the door. I saw… it…" and here Samuel emphasized the word "it" in a cautious whisper as if he was afraid someone might overhear his planned purchase and race him to the store, "in the window yet this morning after I swept Mr. Lloyd's steps so I know it's still there. All my friends think it's the greatest. They keep begging their moms and dads to buy it for them. But so far…well, I just don't think I should wait any long…have you seen how shiny it is? And the color is my very best favorite and…and all those stars…and…well, it's just what I have alllllways, alllllways waaanted."

The three last words came out slowly and elongated, with a pause between each "allllways" as if to confirm the fact to his mother and to himself that a long awaited dream was about to come true.

"Well, you know what Samuel? I think you're absolutely right," KayLee agreed in a serious tone that belied the smile hidden behind her expressionless face. "I don't think we should wait around even one more minute, not even for cookies and milk, but if you don't mind eating a cookie without the milk, why don't I just get one off the pan while you gather up everything from the table, and you can eat it on our way to the hardware store. I believe there's one blue Stargazer just waiting for one special little boy to pay a visit. It's been sitting in that window all by itself long enough.

I'm sure this is the exact right time to find it a new home."

—

As mother and son left the modest bungalow to make their way down the sidewalk to the village's main street, KayLee found herself increasing her pace with each step she took in order to keep up with her child who was nearly running full speed in anticipation of what lay ahead. He turned around one time to be sure she was following him. There was a glow of anticipation on the boy's cheeks and they became more flushed and freckle-spattered as the tin-shingled building that held the long desired prize came closer into view.

KayLee's thoughts wandered back to all the times she and Samuel had gone shopping for groceries at Mr. Lloyd's store and the pattern that had followed thereafter. Having completed their task they would walk over to stand in front of the wide display window of the hardware store that stood adjacent to the grocer's shop. They would gaze in awe at the "two-wheeler" the young boy dreamily hoped to claim as his own one day.

KayLee's heart filled with pride, love, and a touch of sadness as she remembered the one particular day the two of them had stood before the window and while viewing the bicycle the mother had listened to her child vow that someday it would belong to him. He would save all his birthday money, his small allowances, any pennies he would be lucky enough to find on the sidewalk, whatever he had would be put away in his special peanut butter jar until he had the needed amount to make his dream purchase.

Seeing the determined enthusiasm on her son's face as he made this declaration, KayLee couldn't help but be drawn into the same mode of resolution and spoke up with what she considered an intended goal that could involve teamwork. She had told her son that if he could save half of the amount needed to buy the bicycle, she would save aside some money from her teacher's salary check every month. After paying out the sum needed for the regularly scheduled bills there wouldn't be a great deal left over but with a little more strict budgeting she would find a way. With this plan, hopefully before too long they would have enough savings between the two of them to remove the Stargazer from its place in the window and bring it to the bungalow whose kitchen windows were presented with a view of Eden's Wood's, aptly named for the peaceful atmosphere that prevailed as one walked along the paths that wove gently around the regal oaks and graceful pines.

But after KayLee had presented her offer, Samuel had looked up at her, his blue eyes veiled with sincere determination and in a statement laced with an intellect that stretched far beyond his youthful years, said thank you for offering, but if it was all right with her he thought it was about time he started earning money of his own if he wanted to buy grown-up things.

The seriousness with which Samuel had said these words to her, had left KayLee speechless and the pang she felt in her chest told her that what she had known would some day happen was now becoming a reality. Her child would grow up. He would become independent. But at six years old? Surely this was much too soon for him to be thinking and acting like an adult. She wanted him to remain a child. Innocent. Protected from the harshness of life's realities. And yet she knew in her heart she should be proud that her son was already accepting personal responsibility. And what was even more astonishing for someone his age was that he seemed to realize there was a rewarding pride attached to the fact that one had used personally earned finances to make desired purchases. So instead of persisting with the suggestion of her monetary assistance, KayLee had pushed aside her instinct to rescue the situation and let her son's decision go forward.

And it had all happened as if by predetermined act that Samuel's plan could take form.

It had been several months ago when they were again on one of their routine shopping trips to Mr. Lloyd's. KayLee had been preparing batter to make pancakes for her son's lunchtime treat. Samuel had decided he could maybe use a change from his usual noontime request for a peanut butter and jelly sandwich. "I think pancakes would really feel good in my tummy," he had said while rubbing over the area where he planned to store them. When KayLee had gone to get flour from the bin in the pantry cupboard, she saw that it was nearly empty and that there wouldn't be enough for the pancakes or any other baking she might do that day, so there would have to be a hasty trip to the store before a waiting tummy could be pleased.

Arriving at the store, KayLee had gone to the center aisle and removed from the shelf the familiar white paper bag with the blue lettering that held her needed staple. While she was occupied with her shopping, Samuel had made his way to his favorite shelf in the store. His purchase was a carefully chosen special treat from the array of candy boxes displayed near the checkout counter. His hands-down favorite was a rectangular-shaped caramel sucker whose famous yellow and brown wrapper was easily recognized by the eager eyes of any six-year-old little boy. This chewy selection was once again his unanimous choice for this day after very little debate. Quite truthfully, as always, there had been really no debate...just the usual stroll past all the open boxes until he reached the desired one. The two shoppers then had placed their purchases on the linoleum-covered counter and after paying the grocer made ready to return to the waiting batter.

As KayLee and Samuel opened the door to go out, the rusty spring that held the screen door to the wooden doorframe, made a creaking noise. A large cat who was taking his midday nap on the sunlit top step of the entrance, awoke suddenly, no doubt from the noisy intrusion to his resting spot, and let out a loud screeching meow, startling KayLee, causing her to drop her parcel of groceries. The flour bag broke open when it hit the cement threshold, spilling the white powder down the steps and onto the bordering sidewalk. The scattering particles turned the summer scene into one resembling a sudden winter snowfall, and simultaneously turned the silky black cat into a sneezing white phantom.

Mr. Lloyd had come out immediately upon witnessing the commotion to make sure no one was injured and then seeing that there were no consequences except for a very put-out feline, went back inside to retrieve a broom from the storage closet to clean up the spilled flour.

After returning to the powder-covered threshold, the proprietor took only a few sweeps at the dusty residue before stopping abruptly. Glancing briefly at the two spectators who stood beside him, making sure their attention was on his task at hand, as it was indeed, he then reached one arm around to his back and massaged it gently, while making soft moaning sighs with each motion.

"Oh, my. Oooh, my. I do believe this ancient back of mine is telling me it's just can't handle this kind of work anymore. It doesn't seem to have the "springabilty" it used to have. Much as I hate to admit it, I think that old rascal called aging is putting its lasso around me. It certainly looks as if that might just be the case here. I suppose it eventually happens to everyone at some time or other, but I'm afraid my turn has come up sooner than I expected. I'm beginning to think it just might be time for me to start looking around for someone younger to take over this broom job for me." As he spoke the words of feigned surrender, adding a few more somewhat exaggerated moans and groans to the confession, the plotting grocer looked up at KayLee and with a wink said, "Mrs. McQuinn, would you by any chance happen to know where I might find a nice young man, and oh, yes, I must add to that requirement, a reliable one? I'd need someone I can count on to be available mornings to sweep up my steps and maybe do a few other light chores for me every day. I really think it's time I hire an assistant to help me out."

KayLee bent her left arm at the elbow and placed it over her waistline. Clenching her palm, she rested her right elbow on the closed hand, placing her index finger against her cheek as if to ponder the question. Out of the corner of her eye she saw her young son sidle over to her and felt a soft tap on her arm. Holding back the smile that was trying to erupt, she looked down into the wide eyes of her son as he stared back at her and nonchalantly said to him, "Just a minute Samuel, I'm trying to think of someone for Mr. Lloyd."

This time the tap was firmer, more insistent, and as her arm was being pulled downward she suddenly found herself facing one very freckle-spattered cheek. In a whisper no doubt intended to be a hushed refrain, but rather came out quite loud since it was filled with exuberant anticipation (and of course overheard easily by the conspiring storekeeper), Samuel said excitedly, but at the same time a little breathless, "You don't have to think, mommy. He's right here." Pointing his finger to his chest, he added, "I'm the young man he could have. I'm the one." There was no holding back his mounting enthusiasm.

KayLee adopted a look of complete surprise. Then lowering her own voice to a whisper, KayLee leaned forward and cupping her hand next to her son's ear said, "Oh, Samuel, I should have thought of that myself. That's a wonderful idea. How grown-up of you to offer Mr. Lloyd your help. But you know it's a very big responsibility. Mr. Lloyd will need to know he can depend on you every morning. Do you think you're ready for such an important job?" Trying to restrain herself from going over to Mr. Lloyd and giving him a big hug for the joy that was now lighting up her child's eyes, KayLee took a deep, slow breath, willing herself to keep her own fervent emotions under wraps.

Turning his back at an even sharper angle away from Mr. Lloyd, Samuel whispered once again to his mother in what he considered a most hushed tone. This time, though, the words came out louder than the previous ones had, no doubt due to the bottled up excitement that was threatening to overflow like an erupting volcano to the sidewalk and down along the passing street.

Nearly breathless by now, Samuel spilled the words out into the sunny display of midday warmth. "Mommy, ('Mommy?' The retrieved name didn't bypass KayLee's ears) this is just what I need. Remember what's in the window over there?" With these words Samuel nodded his head toward the building next door, as if afraid to say it out loud and risk the chance of revealing what he considered a most darkly shaded secret. Following his motion, KayLee looked over toward the hardware store. Her eyebrows lifted in responsive surprise as if her mind had just been juggled into remembrance. The vision of the two-wheeler, of course, had taken up permanent residence wherever her thoughts had gathered the past several months.

Turning her attention once again to the waiting storekeeper, KayLee spoke in a voice that, while sounding clear and sure, still had beneath its surface a modicum of hesitancy. That natural instinct that clings on tightly making it difficult for a parent to take the next step forward into a new phase of a child's life, and seems to pick up perpetual strength as the goal becomes closer, was pushing ahead to form a blockade to the intruding reality. But seeing the proud, eager look on her son's face, KayLee knew there was no turning back the clock. Time goes forward. So willing herself to join her son in this next phase of his growing up years, she swallowed the lump that had settled in her throat and spoke with a beaming ray of assurance for her young child's offered plan.

"Well, Mr. Lloyd, I think my little boy here knows someone who might be just the one you're looking for." Trying again to keep her tone casual, KayLee watched as Samuel took the few steps needed to stand next to the grocer, who now had his head tilted to one side, eyebrows arched as if waiting in anticipation for a solution to what appeared to be a recently discovered problem.

As the gap between mother and son grew wider and the space between the young boy and older man shortened, Samuel reached out his hand toward the man and said, "I think I'm the assistant you're looking for, Mr. Lloyd. And if you could shake my hand I think we can work something out. You need some help and I need a job. Isn't that right, Mommy?" Again the retreated word. Samuel turned around to face his mother, and in his determination to carry through the plan he had told her about and having now found the way to do so, he saw only the smile on his mother's face. He missed the sound of her pressing heartbeat and the sight of her tears as she nodded, unable to speak any words.

Later on that afternoon after Mr. Lloyd and Samuel had set up a schedule for the times Samuel would come to help him, Mr. Lloyd had telephoned KayLee to make certain that it was indeed all right with her that Samuel come to the store for a short time each day. He then had proceeded to tell her that he had been planning for some time now to offer Samuel some light tasks, but just hadn't known how to approach the situation. This noon's mishap had provided the needed opportunity and he went on to say that today was the first and only time he had been pleased to have had that pesky old cat on his entry steps.

—

Mr. Lloyd had seen Samuel standing by the hardware store window nearly every day for some time now, staring with longing at the bright blue bicycle and knew with KayLee's situation it would no doubt be a while before the purchase could be made. He really could use a little help around the store and Samuel was such a special little boy, maybe a little too sad sometimes (he often thought the same of the lad's mother, but would never say so). And best of all, it would add a sparkle to his day having a young boy like Samuel around the store.

He would give him simple tasks such as sweeping the steps and maybe filling the fruit bins each morning the new shipments came in. He could find simple, non-strenuous tasks for him to do. Not having children of his own, it would be as much a treat for him as it would be a solution to Samuel's plan to obtain the much desired bicycle all by himself. He even had Mrs.

Lloyd sew up a small grocer's apron for Samuel to wear so as to make the lad feel he was really an official helper.

When Samuel came into the store each morning, the first thing he would do was, of course, say "Good morning" to Mr. Lloyd, but then would walk directly to the back room and remove his apron from the nail that Mr. Lloyd had pounded into the beam that was positioned for support in the center of the delegated storeroom. Misjudging Samuel's height, the grocer had placed the nail slightly out of Samuel's reach, so after watching the young boy stretch up on his tiptoes to get the apron each morning, the considerate merchant had remarked that he would lower the nail so Samuel could grasp the apron more easily. But Samuel had insisted he leave it just where it was, after all, he had said proudly, "My mommy says I'm growing more and more each day, so I'm sure that it will be just at the right height very soon. And besides, I'm sure the reaching and stretching will help me grow even faster." So the nail had stayed where it was.

And Samuel had been right. It wasn't long before he was removing the apron while standing with his feet flat on the floor and the excitement in the boy's voice as he had told Mr. Lloyd the good news, had filled the elder grocer with a pride that spread a warm feeling throughout his whole being.

But after Samuel had reached the set height goal, Mr. Lloyd had felt a loss. He missed the squeals of delight that had come from behind the gathered curtain every morning Samuel discovered he was getting taller. So one morning before Samuel arrived at the store, Mr. Lloyd went into the back room of the marketplace. Stretching his arms to their greatest extension, he grasped the rope handle of the small wooden toolbox that sat on a shelf above the egg-candling table. Why he kept it nearly out of reach puzzled him every time he needed it, but he never took the time to move it elsewhere. He set the rectangular box down on the deeply scarred countertop, an irregularly hewn chunk of pine that in his estimation was about the same age he was; thereby it could definitely be labeled an antique!

Releasing the two metal latches that were on the front side of the box, he lifted the lid. The first thing that caught his eye was a flat marking pencil whose painted advertising label was flaking off from years of use. Mentally filling in a few missing letters he concluded that it was a Supersweet Feed advertising token. Next to be lifted out of its resting place was a metal tape measure that had been given to customers by the Central Lumber Company one Christmas several decades ago. He removed a hammer, whose wooden handle was worn smooth and shiny and in the process of rescuing a wayward nail, had lost one of its curved claws. Laying it beside the toolbox, he continued his search.

Shoving aside a pair of rust-coated needle nosed pliers, the grocer couldn't help but wonder what kind of fan-tailed Moby Dick had been attached to the eight-inch fishhook clutched within its pincers. The hook was twice as long as any fish he'd ever seen brought to shore from the Cannon River, the local bullhead infested waters.

Finally he found the object of his scavenger hunt...a three-penny nail. The point was somewhat worn, but Mr. Lloyd's trusty hammer never failed. When duty called, success prevailed. The spike would be driven home!

Walking over to the central beam, the grocer, now turned carpenter, measured two inches above the present nail, using the space between the first and second knuckle of his right index finger to get the exact distance…no point in using a tape measure when there was one attached so conveniently to one's body! The storekeeper then proceeded to pound the slender steel peg into place, leaving the first in its original position. How can you remove anything that held so many happy memories? Then grasping the apron by its neckband, Theodore Lloyd hung the cherished cloth protector on the new nail. After returning the hammer to the toolbox and the toolbox to its proper place, well, to the place it had been anyway, the grocer walked out to the front of the store and waited for Samuel to come to work.

As he counted the day's starting change in the cash register, the proprietor heard the familiar squeak of the screen door and looked up as Samuel entered the quiet store. Receiving the customary 'Good Morning' from his miniature grocer, Mr. Lloyd returned the greeting and struggling to contain the smile that was threatening to escape, he waited for the reaction that would hence be coming from the back room. Another goal and a new challenge to look forward to each starting day.

The sound that erupted the solitude, though, wasn't the one he had expected. Mr. Lloyd had thought Samuel would realize what his fellow grocer had done and why, and would be filled with enthusiasm and bubbling excitement, but the sound that came from the back room was anything but delightful. It was one of considerable despair and mounting disbelief. He no longer heard Samuel's cheerful 'good morning' voice, but rather the sound of fear. "How can this be? Mr. Lloyd, come quick. Something terrible has happened."

Dropping the change he had been counting, not concerned that the copper and silver pieces were now rolling in myriad directions over the counter and onto the linoleum-covered floor within the checkout area, the frightened grocer ran quickly toward the back of the store and pushed aside the striped curtain that hung from a wooden rod across the narrow doorway.

Feeling as if his heart would pop out from his chest, he quickly ran to Samuel's side to see what mishap had occurred to so upset the child. "Samuel, what is it? Are you hurt? Did you fall?"

"No, Mr. Lloyd. It's worse than that. It's... it's terrible. I...I...I don't understand. You know how big I've been getting since I got here?" Nodding his head up and down while he spoke as if to reassure himself that he was growing taller, (the nail had proven that, hadn't it?), Samuel paused to take a deep breath. He tried to continue, but a few random tears were flowing down his cheeks and he had to stop talking so he could wipe them away. Then just as suddenly as he had stopped talking, he started once again. This time, though, each word he uttered came out at a turtle's pace and he spoke as if in a daze.

"Mr. Lloyd, it's terrible, terrible," he went on, eyes not focusing on anything in the room, but rather darting aimlessly about. "Not only have I stopped growing, I'm even shrinking. Look." Turning around toward the apron that was still hooked on the nail,

Samuel reached up to remove it, but couldn't unhook it without stretching and standing on his tiptoes.

A sick feeling dropped to the pit of Mr. Lloyd's stomach as he saw the fear that shadowed his small assistant's face. He had assumed that Samuel would realize what had been done, but not having been around children much, the man obviously was not accustomed to the vulnerable, unseasoned workings of an innocent child's mind. Their immature patterns of thinking would not focus on the fact that there might be a logical reason for a change in routine. Their youthful minds saw only the obvious, and it was obvious to Samuel that if he had reached the apron yesterday, he should be able to reach it today and if he couldn't, well, then, something was dreadfully wrong. He was most very certainly shrinking!

Going quickly to the apron and removing it from the nail, Mr. Lloyd pointed to the lower nail and then hung the apron on it. Kneeling down, and holding onto Samuel's rigidly postured shoulders, the grocer looked into the tear-filled blue eyes of the little boy who was now at his own eye level and with his heart in his throat said in a sad, apologetic voice, "Oh, Samuel, I am so sorry. I should have told you that I put up a new nail and moved the apron to it. What kind of webs do I have blocking up this old head anyway? You aren't getting shorter. The nail is higher. I have so enjoyed watching you grow to reach the apron without a struggle and now that you have done that, I hated to give up the daily excitement of your progress, so I raised the apron in order for us to continue the watch."

Still holding on to the fragile shoulders of his tiny assistant, Theodore Lloyd felt them settle to a more relaxed position in response to the elder grocer's disclosure. A splash of relief washed across the freckled face that was now only inches from the man's contrite one. Suddenly two small arms reached forward and came around Mr. Lloyd's neck, issuing what could only be described as a giant bear hug. Fear no longer mingled with Samuel's words as his mouth settled next to his mentor's ear.

"Thank you, thank you, Mr. Lloyd. I'm...I'm sor...sorry for how I acted, but I was sooo scared. I thought for sure I was shrinking. After all I've gone through to grow, I just couldn't believe it." Samuel leaned back, looking directly into the grocer's face. The boy's eyes widened as he recalled the sacrifices he had been subjected to in the past weeks.

"Do you know how many helpings of carrots and those awful green beans I have had to eat just because mommy said they'd help me grow up big and strong? All I could think of when I couldn't reach my apron was that I had forced them down for nothing!" A brief sniffle followed the anxiety-filled statement.

At a time when a smile would have been the result of the child's declaration, Mr. Lloyd remained in a self-chastising state. He stood once more to his full 5 feet 7 inches and spoke dejectedly. "Samuel, it is I who should be sorry, not you. I should have told you what I had done. You see my mind no longer thinks like the trusting mind of a child and you know I would never do anything to hurt or frighten you. I thought...well, that's my problem. I think too much sometimes. I'm getting to be a real...a...a real dittzlehead."

Brushing aside the puzzled look on Samuel's face, the grocer continued with his confession, feeling more penitent with each word he spoke. "I'm so, so sorry and I apologize again for not telling you. I promise and cross my heart," (he paused to make an X mark over his chest before going on) "not to make any more changes in the store before checking with you. Is that a deal?" Extending a hand toward his little helper, the senior grocer felt the miniature palm join his larger calloused one and watched, with a lump in his throat, as it moved up and down sealing their pact.

Releasing the handshake, the grocer gave Samuel a broad smile and Samuel returned one of his own as a remaining tear escaped to fall on his Mickey Mouse t-shirt. Turning once again toward the beam that held the white apron, Samuel stretched up to remove it from the nail, and then facing Mr. Lloyd with a gleam in his bright blue eyes, said confidently and with a pending promise, "I don't think it will be too long before you're going to have to move that nail up again, Mr. Lloyd. I had broccoli for supper last night." The faces of both grocers, junior and senior, took on the scrunched appearance of a dried prune as the vision of the flowery green vegetable passed before their eyes.

—

As KayLee and Samuel approached the block of local businesses on this long-awaited day, KayLee found herself having to quicken her pace even more than she had been to keep up with Samuel There was no doubt he had set a new speed record for a two block run as they closed in on the gray clapboard building. They had to go past Mr. Lloyd's market before getting to the prized feature window of Mr. Shultz' store and as they drew near the familiar screen door entrance, Samuel paused mid-run. Looking into the window, he stretched his neck about so he could see around the funny looking foot that was perched there. Standing right next to the display was Mr. Lloyd, who had been watching the pair as they made their way onto the main street of the village on their hastened trip to purchase the reward Samuel had earned.

Seeing the grocer standing there, Samuel's face took on a glow that would have put the sun in second place. He held up the bag of treasures while nodding his head and shouting, "I've got it, Mr. Lloyd. I've got enough. We're going to get my Stargazer!"

The pause at the food store lasted only a split second. The last few words faded into the air as Samuel went out ahead of his mother. Reaching his destination, the boy stopped at the base of the steps. Instead of walking into the store he walked past the raised entrance and went over to the large front window. Leaning over he pressed his nose up against the reflecting plate glass and peered inside. His gaze fell upon the coveted star-spangled object that had been the main attraction in what had seemed to be an eternity of dreams for one freckle-faced little boy.

KayLee watched as Samuel left the window to run up the two wide cement steps fronting the store entrance. Turning back around to glance once again at the man standing near the infamous foot display, KayLee saw that the grocer was now walking toward the back of the store, holding the bottom of his apron up to his eyes. She felt a catch in her throat at the vision before her and thought of the caring generosity this dear man had shared with her and her son. She knew now that her decision to remain in Morristown to raise her child after her devastating loss had been the right choice.

Taking a deep breath and exhaling slowly, KayLee made the short walk past the grocer's place of business to the hardware store. She grasped the narrow metal handle on the green and yellow painted screen door (the familiar colors of the world-renown John Deere tractor) stepping onto the creaking wooden floor planks just as Samuel approached the checkout counter. Standing on his tiptoes wearing a smile wider than the horizon, the soon-to-be Stargazer owner handed his bag of payment to the formidable hardware store owner.

—

Everett Shultz had over the years remained somewhat of an enigma in this close-knit southern Minnesota community noted for its "Know thy neighbor" motto. He was teasingly called "Old Crusty" by as his loyal farm customers, just because he tried to sound so tough at times when discussing the latest farm problems or the state of the economy, which was never up to satisfaction at any given time. But they knew full well that even though they couldn't seem to completely break through the man's protective outer shell to find the real Everett Shultz, they had visible proof that he was anything but crusty inside. He dispensed a generous dose of liberty when it came to giving the local farmers running credit for their agricultural related purchases. No payments were ever due until after harvest time or after the cattle and hogs had been sold at market. Plus, no one ever received a billing statement. Shultz Hardware used the honor system and it hadn't failed in over 45 years. Every credit slip in the cash register was eventually marked "Paid In Full."

Everett Shultz was as promontory a figure in this small riverside town as were the faces that jutted out from Mt. Rushmore in the Black Hills of South Dakota. He was immediately recognizable anywhere he went by his flowing gray beard, lanky body, and his unrelenting attire. The hardware merchant was unfailingly clad in his trademark blue and gray striped bib overalls…a staple item stocked at his establishment, but one that turned into an "outerwear specialty" when it was sold at an advertised bargain price two times a year. The first sale took place right before spring planting and the second just as the autumn harvest neared.

The utilitarian outfit could be found at the Shultz place of business at the far end of aisle four, top shelf, for the biannual sale price of $4.95 a pair with two extra metal buttons attached at the bottom of the suspender straps just in case one should pop off and get lost. "The Best Bargain In Town"…or so said the weekly Morristown Press ad during the sale weeks.

When the week of planting spring crops ended and the days of harvesting were over, the price on the hand printed sign in aisle four went back up to $4.99. The local farmers chuckled inwardly at the price changes, but in appreciation for the empathy shown toward their earning circumstances, they reciprocated with a good deed of their own. The week after the sales were off, each and every farmer from around the county came into the store to purchase a stiff new pair of the bibbed overall at the higher price. Each patron would slap a crisp five-dollar bill on the counter and tell proprietor Shultz to keep the change. Glances were exchanged as tokens of gratitude and vigorous handshaking replaced the words that the hardy men found difficult to express. Life was good.

As stern looking and sober as Mr. Shultz always appeared outwardly to the townspeople of Morristown, there was a pliable side to the man's nature that was in due course discerned by everyone who came to know him. KayLee found this label duly applied one day not so long ago when she had gone into the hardware store while Samuel was busy filling a bin with freshly arrived apples at Mr. Lloyd's marketplace. She wanted to check on the price of the treasured Stargazer and also felt a need to inquire if it would be possible to order another of the same model should the window display one be purchased by another little boy who was as eager as Samuel to become its owner.

After making her inquiry, Mr. Shultz hadn't answered her right away, but rather had cocked his head, while putting a forefinger across his puckered lips, and proceeded to look around the store as he stood behind the counter. KayLee watched on in puzzlement at the storekeeper's strange actions, but remained silent, engrossed with abiding interest. There seemed to be an act of espionage taking place right before her eyes. The bearded man then came out from behind the counter and made his way up and down the pristine, well-organized aisles. KayLee surmised that he was apparently checking to see if he and "Mrs. McQuinn" (he never called her by her first name, KayLee…never called any of the town ladies by their given names…didn't seem proper or respectful, he would say when questioned about the habit) were the only two occupants in the home/farm supply store.

It wasn't possible from his vantage point at the cash register to see the pint-sized youthful customers who would come into the store and stand (sit was a more accurate position) for hours at the metal toy section, "plowing" across the buckled planks of the warped wooden floor or hauling make-believe loads of gravel from one end of the aisle to the other. Everett Shultz always found himself silently amused when he heard the imitated sounds of a tractor's "putt-putt" or the "rurrn-rurrn" of the sturdy, bright yellow gravel truck.

The soft-hearted proprietor would wait several minutes until the simulated roars faded somewhat and then would ask in as gruff a tone as he could conjure up through his feelings of sated delight, "Are you young ones playing with those toys? If you play with them, you have to buy them you know." A congregation of voices would answer in unison with a highly excited pitch, "No, no, Mr. Shultz, we're…we're only looking. Honest." Of course, the noise that was heard as miniature implements were placed back on the shelf, and the loud whispers of "Hurry, before he sees us," brought a smile to the storekeeper's face that at times was difficult to erase before several little bodies were seen sneaking around the end of the aisle and scooting out the door.

The echoes of, "Hey, you guys, wait for me", lingered in the air long after the elfin figures had gone out the heavy oak door, which because of its cumbersome weight took at least three of the little ones to open…one to press down on the brass latch and two more to pull on the handle to get it open. This of course made the "Wait for me" statement totally unnecessary. They were all trapped at the scene until the last one came to help with the escape. The summer escape route of course was much less complicated than the winter one since there was only the flimsy screen door to go through when making the frantic getaway.

As soon as the solid door latched itself by its spring-loaded closure (or the screen door had slammed loudly) and when the high-ceilinged room had become quiet once again, emptied of its exuberant patrons, the overalls-bedecked clerk would walk over to the toy-filled display shelves, studiously observing which of the replica machinery pieces had been moved and haphazardly replaced by young eager hands. Everett Shultz would then return to the highly varnished wooden checkout counter. Lifting up the cash register drawer, he would take out a discreetly hidden notebook. Using the worn-down point of a stubby lead pencil the retailer would make precise notations from the scene he had just observed. When Christmas or birthday times rolled around for the youngsters of Morristown, parents of the miniature visitors would come to Mr. Shultz asking to see his covert listings and once observed would thereby have a head start on their children's Christmas lists or be delighted to find the solution for a special birthday surprise.

There wasn't a calloused area to be found anywhere on the old gentleman's heart. The townspeople compared him to a well-done roasted marshmallow. Crisp and crackled on the outside, but soft and smooth on the inside. That pretty well described Mr. Shultz, the local hardware man. Of course, having had eleven children of his own and now the grandfather of forty-two and two-thirds grandchildren, one had to admit there was a long train of experience on Everett Shultz' track that helped him read children's utmost wishes and desires.

After making the visual espionage tour of the toy-filled aisles that day while KayLee had waited next to the counter, Everett Shultz, assured that they were indeed quite by themselves, now took on a look of sincere, gentle caring and with a voice that surprised KayLee, since she had only heard about the gruffer version from Samuel (who was told by his friends that you had to be very careful when you were in Mr. Shultz' store and remember to be very quiet when you played with the trucks or the hardware man would really yell), felt her heart fill with tenderness as the man told her he had no intention of selling that blue bicycle to anyone but young Samuel.

"I have watched that young man stare through my window so many times with his dreamy expression of longing, that it would make me feel like the worst sort of ogre if I even let another little boy touch it. It will be in this store, Mrs. McQuinn, until the day I remove it from the display window and give it to your son to take home. Oh, by the way, the price is going down now. It's been here for quite some time, so it's hardly brand new anymore." With that statement, the man rubbed his long beard and turned around and went back to his station behind the checkout counter. "You just let me know when you want it and I'll give it an extra shineup. That's a pretty special boy you have there, Mrs. McQuinn, a pretty special boy."

KayLee had an overwhelming desire to lean over the counter and give the pliant merchant a suffocating hug for all his caring and generosity, but hugging a marshmallow can be a risky matter, so instead she had just whispered a thank you as she turned to leave the store, brushing away a reservoir of unfettered tears. When she felt the sidewalk beneath her feet once again, her legs seemed to pick up speed as if they were propelled by engine force. She couldn't seem to get back to that modest dwelling near the woods fast enough. There was an extra big hug just waiting to be given to a very special little boy once he returned from his morning duties, which when she glanced at her watch noticed it would be in just a few minutes. She wanted to be waiting at the door when he arrived back home.

—

Standing at the window as she watched her son polish, for at least the tenth time, the sky-blue, star-covered bars on his new bicycle, KayLee became aware that the elation she had been filled with only moments ago was slowly trickling away, being replaced with a feeling she wasn't certain she was prepared to face. Her little boy was growing up. First a tricycle, now a bicycle. How far away was getting that first car?

Now she was really getting ahead of things. She scolded herself mentally and watched as Samuel struggled to get his leg over the bar in preparation for that first special ride. Her son had insisted that she stay inside the house until he was sure he could master the deed on his own. Seeing that he wasn't successful the first three times, she smiled to herself and surmised that the trip to Meier's used car lot ("Our 'Seconds' Can Be Your 'Firsts') could be postponed for at least a little while yet.

And then as her thoughts scattered, she heard the delighted squeal of an excited six-year-old as he called for an audience. "Mother. Mother, come look at me. I did it. I'm riding!"

And he was. Well, after a fashion anyway. His posture was such that he looked much like a soft pretzel curved into an irregular shape, his shoulders nearly touching the handlebars. His feet, decked out in dark blue Nikes, tried to remain on the pedals, but a threat was hovering over them offering the temptation to touch the ground for an instant of security.

When coming to the end of the sidewalk, where the concrete ended and the path to the woods began, the novice biker did not apply the brakes, but rather dragged his left foot on the ground to stop his motion. One new thing at a time. Brakes and turning around while moving would have to be added later.

After lifting his right leg to bring it up and over the bicycle seat, Samuel stood at the side of the blue and white challenger. Putting one small hand on the center bracket of the shiny curved handlebar while grasping the triangular cushioned seat with the other, the boy made one careful but deliberate movement and lifted the bicycle a fraction of an inch off the ground. While the two-wheeler wasn't a full-sized model, for a six-year-old it was awkward to move and a bit of a challenge weight-wise. Therefore, as Samuel made the turn-around, the back wheel scraped across the cement walkway causing the young boy to raise his shoulders and gasp with concern.

Glancing down at the wheel to see if there was any sign of irreparable damage to what he considered a delicate piece of equipment, he found he could only look at the outer rim of the tire. He was holding the bicycle up with both hands and didn't want to let go of the secure grip he had on it to check the bottom tread. When assured that all was well, within his limited range of observance, he once again took a riding position atop the revered vehicle.

He repeated the identical riding, stopping, turning pattern several times more until he felt he had it mastered and then, pausing at the end of the walkway that fronted the white bungalow, he got down off the bicycle and with his right foot lowered the silver-colored kickstand to its bracing position. He then ran up the sidewalk and into the house.

"Did you see me, Mother, did you? I didn't tip over even once." Enthusiasm threaded through each word the young boy uttered as he made his way to the kitchen where his mother was washing and drying the last of the baking dishes. "I just knew that bicycle was meant for me. It's really easy to ride. I think I did extra, extra good for someone only six years old, don't you, Mother?" Astonishment as well as pride worked its way through the erupting voice.

KayLee was certain that Samuel hadn't taken even one breath during his whole speech. Laying the large white dishtowel on the counter top next to the sink, she leaned down and wrapped her arms around her son as he came next to her. Displaying a look of utter amazement, she assured her young son that she was certain no other six-year-old had ever mastered a two-wheeler as quickly as he had. Without a doubt, he had learned to ride a bicycle faster than any other person in the whole state of Minnesota and maybe the whole world. The freckled cheeks of the now proclaimed seasoned rider began to take on the deepened colors of an autumn sunset with each issued compliment. This would be a day to remember far beyond all other memories...for more reasons than the one that had just taken place.

Releasing the hold on her son, KayLee rose and stepped back a short pace from the child. Raising her eyebrows while folding her arms in front of her, she said to the energy sparked boy who remained in perpetual motion, "Well now. I do believe this big event calls for a celebration, don't you, young man?"

The bouncing body stopped in mid-bounce. "Young...young man?" Samuel's eyes widened at the words. "Is...is that what I am...now that I can ride a bicycle? A young man? Samuel's eyes opened even wider, his mouth dropping open as if this new title plus learning how to ride a two-wheeler all in one day, was just about more excitement than one small boy could handle.

"Well, I would certainly think so. That was quite an accomplishment in such a short time. And now, I wouldn't be surprised if I could find a few cookies in the pantry for someone who has had such a big day. How does that sound?"

"That's the second best sound I've heard all day, Mother," Samuel said as he climbed onto the chair at

51

the table in anticipation of the treat he was about to devour.

"And what is the *best* sound you've heard today, if you don't mind me asking?" Tilting her head to the side, her eyes harboring a quizzical look, KayLee turned and while waiting for his answer, walked into the pantry. Returning to the kitchen area, she took a plate from the cupboard, put the two chocolate chip cookies on it and carried the treat to the table, setting the plate in front of Samuel who had quit bouncing long enough to sit down for his snack.

Walking over to the refrigerator, she took out a half-gallon container of milk and poured the cold white liquid into Samuel's favorite cup, the one that had Winnie the Pooh and his famous honey pot on the front. She carried the drink over to her son.

With Samuel threatening to swallow the whole cup of milk in one gulp, KayLee interrupted the gesture by asking him a question. "Samuel, did you answer my question?" She thought she had heard a stifled mumble while standing behind the open refrigerator door, but when she had looked toward the table Samuel was putting a cookie in his mouth so surmised she had been mistaken.

"Maybe you should finish that cookie before you say anything." KayLee smiled as she noticed both cookies were already gone and her son's cheeks were puffed out like a squandering chipmunk that had just gathered a season's worth of seeds.

"I'm...I'm sorry", were the only words Samuel managed to get out before taking the last swallow of milk. "Those cookies were really good. I think I could probably get down a couple more. Anyway, what I said was that I was surprised at your question, you know asking me about the best sound that I had heard today." Samuel went on with his explanation as his mother made a return trip to the pantry and the refrigerator. "I thought you would know without asking. But then I guess sometimes kids can figure things out quicker than adults." There was no pause to allow for his mother's reaction to that statement, which was just as well, since KayLee was stunned speechless, wondering how a six-year-old had come to that conclusion. The boy continued as his mother came around the counter.

"It was when I dumped all the coins on Mr. Shultz' counter and it was the exact amount I needed to buy my Stargazer. It was the best sound I have ever, ever heard." Samuel's face lit up as if he were a string of Christmas lights, his eyes glowing like fireflies on a warm summer night.

The sudden hint of soft laughter that came from his mother as he gave his answer, caused Samuel to look up suddenly and he forgot about the bicycle, the cookies…everything was pushed back from his mind except for the sound he had just heard. He stared at his mother who was now standing on the opposite side of the table from where Samuel was sitting. He found himself unable to say any more words.

Noticing the abrupt insertion of silence, KayLee paused with the milk carton and the plate of cookies she had refilled by request. Seeing the strange look on her son's face, her hand released its tight hold on the plate. It fell out of her hand, landing on the table breaking the dish and sending the cookies rolling across the table surface. The sound of the plate shattering instinctively tightened the grasp of her other hand and she shakily set the milk container down on the table not taking her glance off the startled look of the face that sat silently staring at her.

Coming around to the side of the table where her son was sitting, she finally broke the pervading silence. "What is it, Samuel? Don't you feel well?" Reaching out she pressed her hand to her child's forehead to see if he had suddenly come down with a fever. She had read somewhere in one of her parenting magazines that extreme excitement could do that to a child.

"I…I'm all right, Mother. I was…I was just…just thinking…ah…maybe…maybe I should move my Stargazer closer to the house. I…I…wouldn't want anything to happen to it while I'm…I'm in here having cookies. I'll be…I'll be right back." With that, Samuel quickly slid off the cushion-covered chair and ran out of the room toward the front door.

Shaking her head as she watched Samuel leave the room, she felt the frown on her brow deepen. What had brought that on so suddenly? What had come about to change her son from a bubble of enthusiasm to someone who looked so completely puzzled and confused?

Walking to the living room and looking out the door toward the sidewalk, KayLee saw her son standing next to the blue and white bicycle, but he wasn't bringing it closer to the house, at least not just yet. He was standing next to it with his head bent forward. She watched as his hand came up behind his head. His hand moved side to side as he rubbed the back of his neck. Turning his head toward the house, KayLee saw a most bewildered look on the child's face and wondered what had happened to bring on such a complete turnaround. It was almost as if he had seen or heard something totally foreign or unexpected but couldn't quite figure out what it was. If KayLee had known the thoughts that were tumbling throughout her young son's mind, she would have been deeply disturbed and saddened.

Now he was sure of it. It was so close. She had almost done it, Samuel thought as he stood on the cemented walkway. It was close, but still not there. If only... The child had known for a long time that something very important was missing, missing from his days, missing from his nights, missing. But until a few minutes ago, while sitting at the table, he hadn't realized how often he thought about it. It must be right there all the time...waiting. And now she, his mother, had brought the memory so close to the surface, he could feel it trying to escape. Was it a missing sound? Was that what he was searching for? When *he* was here did she...did they...?

Samuel shook his head as if trying to set free a caged memory, but the bonds were still too securely locked. He knew he had heard it one time, long ago, but it no longer surrounded him so he didn't know for certain if he'd even recognize it if he did hear it. But if he just listened more carefully...maybe. If only he had a father, maybe he would help him look for it.

—

"Samuel, your milk is getting warm. Are you coming back in to finish it?" KayLee watched as Samuel jumped suddenly from the sound of her voice. Not knowing just exactly what had taken place at the table, she decided to act natural, and if he were troubled about something, he would tell her. That was one thing she could count on, although at times he seemed to withdraw into himself as if searching for something not quite near enough to grasp. When she would try to ask him about his silence he would just say, "Oh, Mother, I'm just trying to stretch my thinking cap so it doesn't get too small." And he would smile a half smile, not entirely convincing a weary mother, but she would let it go by and hug him tightly. More tightly than was comfortable for someone so small, but he felt it was something she needed as much as he did…a child's senses sometimes being more alert than an adult's.

Turning around to face his mother, he smiled a not-too-convincing smile, but it was there nonetheless. "Could you put it in the refrigerator, Mother? I'm kinda full right now." Rubbing his hand across his tummy area as if to persuade the issue, he added, "I'll finish it later, okay?"

"Of course, that would be just fine, Samuel, but I thought you were…" She was interrupted by her son's voice as he seemed to change his demeanor right before her eyes.

A look of excitement and anticipation appeared once again to cover the puzzled look of only moments ago and the bounce seemed to be returning quickly to his movements. "Mother, since I'm so good at riding now, could I…that is…would it be okay if I just go for a short, short ride on the path through the woods? I promise not to go far. I just want to practice a little more. Could I please? Pleeeease?"

KayLee was already shaking her head "no" before Samuel spoke the last word. But hearing the drawn out final plea, she felt herself questioning her initial reaction. Perhaps she was too overprotective. She couldn't help it. Not after what she had been through. But, really when she took a second to rationalize the request, the woods was only a few steps from the edge of the sidewalk and she and Samuel had walked along the wooded path nearly every day since he had learned to walk.

With that memory taking root in KayLee's thoughts, her mind jaunted back to the times the three of them had enjoyed the peacefulness of those same woods. The three of them...how long ago that seemed. Shaking her head, she quickly dismissed the clouded picture, it's memory still too painful even after these several years. She had to let him try new things some time, didn't she? She couldn't hold him back forever. But now?

"Oh, Samuel, I don't...ah...I ...I think...ah..." here KayLee paused to take a deep breath before continuing, the feeling of cautious reluctance somewhat abating, then went on, "I...oh, dear..." another pause and then, "Yes, yes...I think that would be a very good place to practice Samuel, why don't you do that." she said, trying to sound more reassuring than she actually was feeling.

Catching her son off guard, who was already practicing his next plea, she held back the smile that she felt moving across her face.

"But, Mother, how will I ever learn to...what? I...I can do it? I can really ri...ride into the...the woods?" Samuel was so surprised at her answer he was nearly at a loss for words, which was a miracle in itself for a six-year-old.

"Yes, Samuel, you may, but don't go too far. Just go to the first set of feeders and turn around. All right?"

—

The feeders. That was a mystery in itself. One day they had just appeared. There were tall ones and short ones. Some on the ground for the shorter-legged creatures. Trays of shelled corn for the deer who roamed freely and safely among the trees. Salt and mineral blocks placed on tree stumps. And bird feeders for every variety of species that occupied the dense woods. Suet containers for woodpeckers, ground feeders for cardinals, hanging ones for chickadees, nuthatches, finches. Everything with wings could find appropriate dining at its particular feeding station. And the squirrels, of course, felt an obligation to visit each and every display of morsels.

No one in the small town knew how the rough-cut stations with their abundant nourishments had gotten there. They seemed to have come out of nowhere. One day there were none and the next they were placed strategically all along the pathway, filled generously to their very edges as they waited for the daily guests to arrive.

—

Climbing onto his bicycle, Samuel turned around before starting on his way. He blew a kiss to his mother as he shouted "thank you" over and over again, vowing he would be an even better rider when he got back. "Just wait and see," he predicted with utmost certainty.

KayLee stood at the door, returning the sentimental gesture, and pondered how the perplexing scene that had just occurred in the modest kitchen had reversed itself and seemed never to have taken place. Shaking her head as she turned around, she went back into the kitchen to pick up the shattered pieces of the plate and to put Samuel's glass of milk in the refrigerator, a refreshment to be finished on his return trip. No doubt there would be an additional cookie treat to keep it company.

While returning the baking utensils to their proper places in the pantry, KayLee started feeling a little uneasy about the decision she had just made. But what could possibly go wrong on one short trip down the pathway? She would have to learn to adjust to all the changes happening now that Samuel was growing up. But, it wouldn't be easy. Not easy at all. She kept reminding herself, as she finished tidying up the dining area, that it was one quick ride in the woods, five minutes at the most. It was a quiet, safe trail. One enjoyed by people of all ages. What could possibly happen to shake up the life she had come to know and accept? What indeed.

—

Starting down the tree-shaded path, the happy rider now seemed to have only one thought on his mind. At last he was the official owner of his very own bicycle.

He had worked hard and saved for so long and finally the day had arrived. It was even more exciting than he had imagined. Sitting up above the ground; the soft breeze blowing in his face as he gained confidence in his skill. He guessed now that he could do or be anything in the world that he wanted. Maybe one day he would be an airplane pilot and be even higher off the ground. Wouldn't that be exciting!

With his daydreams carrying him into the clouds, he became totally unaware of his surroundings. Had he been looking off to the side of the pathway, he would have seen the low branches on the nearby shrubs being separated by a pair of large, but delicate, strong hands. Perhaps he would even have seen the dark eyes that watched him as he moved dreamily along the skyway, or noticed the ears that were bent toward him as he talked to his trusting, make-believe passengers about how high they were flying and that the weather was going to be sunny and bright when they made their landing at Sky Harbor airport.

Those were the words the pilot had announced through the heavy metal walls (more magic?) of the airplane that was taking Samuel and his mother to Arizona last winter so they could spend Christmas with Samuel's grandparents.

Could the pilot's weather forecast actually be true? When they had left Minnesota on that early December morning it was cold and snowy and in only a few hours they were supposed to be walking out into bright skies and warming sunshine? That couldn't be possible…could it? But the captain had been right. In just a few short hours winter had turned to summer.

There were so many delightful surprises in Samuel's world.

—

The hooded eyes that now followed the young boy were not glowing with the joy of watching a child at play, but rather were filled with painful longing, a lingering sadness that could find no means of escape. Memories stirred behind the haunting look. There had been another child. A little boy. He would have been about the same age, had the same burnished tones to his tousled hair, the same rusty color on his cheeks. If only he had...if only they...we could have walked this very path. The three of us. We would have laughed, scattered the leaves about with our feet in the autumn, made tracks in the new-fallen snows of winter. The trees would have sheltered us as we looked across a secluded meadow, watching the animals as they gathered their young to roam freely about their own private playground. One family enjoying another. Equal in their joy. Equal in their freedom.

Hurt, anger, guilt...they had all been so much a part of his life these past years that it was almost too difficult to watch the child and his mother as they had walked this same path so many times. He would feel at those times, as he observed them, that perhaps he kept these feelings at the surface to punish himself for what he had done, or rather not been able to do, those many years ago. What good was all his education, all his training, the learned skills? He'd had it all and still hadn't been able to save his own wife and newborn son.

He had tried these past months, years now, to stay within the densely wooded boundaries of his reclusive one-room log dwelling. But the quiet murmurings of mother and child always brought him to the edge of the walkway. It was as if he were being drawn by an invisible magnet to observe their every move and sound. There was something strange, though, something he noticed each time he saw them. There were never any sounds of joy or laughter as they strolled along each day. Just a quiet, solemn walk. But he could feel the love between them as they walked hand in hand, stopping to smell the wild flowers or lingering under a massive oak to watch a squirrel as it gathered acorns for its winter pantry. And...it was always just the two of them. Was there a...?

There was nothing to be gained by letting his thoughts wander. The life of seclusion he had chosen wasn't just because of his devastating loss but was also the end result of the haunting lack of confidence that had lingered throughout the hours of his days and nights. He felt he would be incapable of ever again helping the sick or injured.

But as he moved about in his secluded surroundings, the forces of nature began to provide outlets for his self-imposed sentence. A need for his healing gifts arose. He found that it wasn't just in a sterile operating room or a well-equipped office setting that his skills could be applied. This new opening for him came to fruition one early evening as he was cutting firewood a short distance from his simple secluded dwelling.

While moving a large, cumbersome log away from a clump of fallen aspens, the adopted woodsman saw a slight movement behind the leafy pile. Gently lowering his long-handled ax to the ground, he had walked cautiously around the splintered timbers. There, nearly hidden beneath one of the decayed white trunks, lay a young deer. Its eyes didn't seem to be filled with daunting apprehension as would be duly anticipated, but rather there appeared in the glazed-over surfaces of its pupils, a deepened shadow of pain.

With trained observance, the man moved slowly but steadily toward the yearling. As he approached the delicate animal, the former medical professional saw that its leg had been caught under one of the larger detached tree branches therefore it was unable to free itself from the entrapment.

The former caretaker of the wounded and infirmed carefully lifted the ponderous branch off the delicate limb. As the weighted piece was lifted free, the young deer had tried to scramble away by moving his uninjured legs frantically over the dampened floor of the shaded woods, but was soon overcome by exhaustion. Surrendering hopelessly to the situation, the woodland creature had laid its head back down on the leaf-strewn ground.

The yearling had no reason to fear the human intruder, for the gentle man who stood over him was not there to harm him, but to rescue, offer comfort, and give him aid. And that was when life had once again found meaning for the dispirited healer who for too long had kept his gift of healing restoration wrapped securely in the bindings of the past.

—

Since that day several years ago, Dr. Markus Garrity had served devotedly a world he would not have discovered had he not retreated so far from life and living. Having chosen not to treat the one species of the earth, he had found another who needed his kindness, his knowledge, his dedication. The present had not removed the feelings of loss and suffering that so deeply rooted the man's past, but it had shed some light on the shadows that seemed to be on every surface of his secluded lifestyle. He had learned how to exist among the creatures that had been on the earth long before the supposedly superior of species had made its debut. After living with and being a close participant in the daily rituals of the animal kingdom, Markus Garrity had come to believe that there was much to be learned from the intelligent, but often complex, creatures that roamed the very earth that man often claimed as his own.

—

After tidying up the kitchen, KayLee decided to step out outside to check on the flowers she had planted around the perimeter of the house. Well, the truth was that she felt more at ease being out in the yard within sight of the path where Samuel would exit from his maiden voyage into the woods. Allowing herself one brief glance toward the narrow roadway, she then turned toward her supposed mission, surveying her amateur landscaping. Noticing that some of the marigolds in the brick-encased flowerbeds bordering the bungalow were wilted, she walked over to the sunburst array of color and leaned over to snap off the shriveled, faded petals.

Making her way around to the side and backyard containers, KayLee stopped suddenly, turning her head in the direction of the woods. Had she heard something? Was someone calling out? "Oh," she thought to herself, "it's probably just some children romping at the nearby playground." When no other sound echoed in the air, she bent down once more to continue the pruning. But as she plucked out another gathering of browned petals, the solitude of the day was interrupted once again. This time the sound was closer and there was no doubt it was coming from the area of the woods. She recognized it as the agonizing cries of a child. Was it…? Samuel? A chill went down her spine as the familiarity of the voice pierced her ears.

Running quickly toward the front yard, she felt a stabbing jolt in the pit of her stomach. She knew the voice. Oh, dear God. Please…no. Please let him be all right.

Just as she came around the corner of the house, KayLee saw Samuel running out of the woods, cutting across the sidewalk onto the lawn in their front yard. No bicycle in sight. Just a little boy with tears streaming down both cheeks, arms flying about aimlessly, and that fear-laced voice calling, "Mommy, mommy where are you? I didn't mean to do it. Mommy? You have to come quick. I didn't see him. I didn't see him at all. One minute he wasn't there and then he…I…I don't want that old bicycle anymore. I hate it. I'm sor… sorry. I'm so sorry. I hurt him, mommy. I really hur...hurt him. Please come quick. Mommy, where are you?"

So distraught was her child that he ran right past her and into the house without realizing she was standing next to the steps that led to the front door. Going quickly up the steps and back to the kitchen where Samuel was still calling "Mommy" (realizing for the first time that her son hadn't said "Mother" while searching for her, but rather had returned to the pre-Bambi title) KayLee felt her heart skip a beat. She had to take a deep, settling breath before speaking. "Oh, Samuel, my dear child," she thought as she saw tears falling down, dampening the dirt-smudged white t-shirt, soaking Mickey Mouse's ears and moistening the pert black bow tie that was the character's trademark, "will life always have these trying moments? Will the days, the years ever get easier?"

Having settled her heart back to its normal rhythm, KayLee rushed toward her young son. "I'm here, sweetheart, what is it? What happened? Are you hurt?" Coming up behind him as he stood near the kitchen table, she put her hands on her son's shoulders and turned him around to face her. Making a brisk over-all assessment of the little boy, KayLee saw no visible signs of injury. No deep scrapes on his tiny arms and legs, just a light coating of dust on his knees and elbows. No cuts or bruises on his face. If he wasn't hurt, then why was he feeling so much pain? Then the words that she had heard him crying out as he had come running into the house began to unravel throughout her mind. It was as if someone had pressed a reset button and the replay was giving her a second chance to try to understand the ensuing situation.

Assured that he had no physical wounds, KayLee now felt a need to move on to her son's apparent emotional injury, for indeed he was suffering from a pain that was every bit as debilitating as any outward sign of trauma would be. "Samuel, slow down, sweetheart. Take a deep breath, okay? And then you can tell me what happened." Since her son seemed incapable of offering any explanation through his lingering sobs, and just didn't seem ready to take a breath, much less a deep one, KayLee tried offering several options of her own to get to the solution of whatever was upsetting her child.

"What…what did you mean when you said, 'you hurt someone'? Did you have an accident with your bicycle? Did you run into someone walking on the path? What happened, Samuel? Can you tell me?"

Finally, after gulping several more overgrown sobs, Samuel took the suggested deep breath and with a quiver in his voice attempted to explain what had happened.

"I…I wa…was riding along down…down the path just thinking and feel…feeling how happy I was to finally have…have my new…new Star…Stargazer, when I thought I…I heard… a…a noise in the bushes beside the trail. I only turned my…my head for a quick…quick second, Mommy, honest I did. Only a little, little second." As the small boy paused to stop an intruding sob, KayLee heard again his reversion to her previous title. "Oh, Samuel, you are such a precious, innocent child," she thought as she watched him struggling with his personal reprimand as he continued with his confession.

"And…and then when I turned back around again, there…there he was, right…right in front of me, chew…chewing on some grass that was in the middle of the path. When I saw him, I couldn't remember how to…how to use the brakes or…or anything. I was so afraid I would hit him. And then it was just like I was in a dream, like one of my bad dreams when it's dark everywhere and suddenly there's something right in front of me and …and I…I can't, couldn't stop."

A bolt from the past hit KayLee, nearly knocking her over. She saw a flash of lightning, drenching rain, bright lights, heard a screeching sound…and then silence prevailed. Life and love, joy and laughter…all dissolving into one crumbled heap of metal…

KayLee felt her body tremble involuntarily as she was brought back to reality as the sorrowful voice of her son pierced through her reverie. "He tried to run, but I think he felt just like I did. Not…not sure what to do or which way to go to be safe, and…well, since neither one of us could think straight we…we…oh, Mommy, I ran over his little leg. I'm so sorry. I'm so sorry. I love animals. I would never hurt any of them on…on purpose. You know that, don't you? The tears now were running in streams across the freckled field, threatening to drown everything they crossed.

"What…what was it, Sam…Samuel? What did you…?" KayLee asked, still reeling from the vision that had pressed its way into the present dilemma. It would take more willpower than she felt capable of releasing at the moment if she was going to try to sound calm for her son's sake. 'Bad dreams'? 'Dark'? 'Something right in front of him'? He couldn't know what… she hadn't told him about the detailed circumstances of the accident, only that... Had he overheard...?

Trying once again to brush aside the haunting memories, and gain control of the emotions that she had so tightly reined in over the past years, KayLee became aware of the additional heartache that was pushing its way into her already overtaxed state of anxiety. Her only child was feeling intense remorse for the suffering he had brought to the small animal that was now lying injured somewhere on the secluded pathway. He needed her guidance, her reassurance.

"It was a little bunny, Mommy, just a scared, fluffy little bunny rabbit," Samuel said, interrupting his mother before she could finish the second question. "He couldn't help it if he was hungry and even...even with his long ears, I guess he...he just didn't hear me. I think he was so happy to have the fresh green grass... they really like grass, you know." With this statement, it seemed Samuel had temporarily forgotten his deep-seated suffering because his eyes lit up as he shared his youthful knowledge about a rabbit's dietary preferences. "It's their favorite, you know. Well, next to lettuce, that is. That's their best favorite." "Anyway," he sighed deeply and then continued with his previous tale, his voice once again returning to its anxious tone and cadence, "I think he was just so busy eating that he must not have heard me coming until I was right...right by him." Again, a choking sob escaped as the entire scene played over in the boy's mind. Two small hands went up to brush back some of the delinquent tears that chose to continue erupting, and a dirt-covered sleeve was stretched out to serve as a blotter for one dripping, freckled nose.

"Mommy, please, we have to go back there. Now. Before... Come with me," her son begged as he reached for his mother's hand, "We have to see if we can help him. I tried to lift him up to let him try out his leg, but he just flopped down every time I set him up. Maybe we can bring him back and find someone to help fix him." He pulled on his mother's hand, urging her silently with his eager footsteps toward the direction of the front door.

"Of course, Samuel, we'll go right away. Just grab the blue blanket that's on the sofa. That will give us something to wrap him in so he stays warm. Sometimes when people or animals get hurt they feel cold and shivery. We'll want him to be comfortable. Then we'll come back and take him to Mr. Lloyd's store. He may know someone who can help fix the injured leg. He seems to know so many people, I'm sure he'll be able to tell us what to do."

Hurrying through the kitchen, across the shiny wooden floors of the cozy living room and out the screen door, mother and son moved quickly toward the wooded trail, the small boy clutching the soft blanket close to his body, already into the shaded area and heading down the path before his mother had left the cemented walkway.

As KayLee reached the area where the mishap had taken place, marked acutely by the overturned blue and white Stargazer, she saw her child rushing from one side of the trail to the other, pulling back the long weeds and looking very distressed and confused.

"What is it, Samuel?" She said as she looked down at the deserted pathway, a feeling of dread coming to the surface.

"He's...he's not... here, Mommy. I can't find him anywhere. I don't understand. He couldn't go anywhere. I told you I tried to get him to stand, but...but his leg was just too wobbly. Do you think some big...bigger animal...oh, Mommy. I shouldn't have left him alone. What if something happened to...?"

"Samuel, look! Over here." KayLee interrupted her son's fearful prediction, waving her arm to direct him to come over toward her. Holding aside some feathery crowned flowers that were on the opposite side of the path from where Samuel stood, KayLee peered down and there, sleeping in the protected area, was a tiny, silent bundle of gray fur. Samuel came rushing to his mother's side and as he looked down where she pointed, he, too, saw what she had uncovered. The helpless victim of the unfortunate incident.

A miniature ball of fluff began to expand as if hatching from a shelled domain. As it stretched forth, a quartette of legs popped out from the puff of fur and both onlookers released a gasp as the leg that had been resting nearest to the downy soft bedding, came out from beneath the pale gray coat. But the leg wasn't gray. It was white! A flat piece of manila colored wood with rounded ends lay against the injured limb and a strip of white cloth was wrapped loosely around it to hold the brace securely in place. Somehow, the fragile leg had been tended to, temporarily mending the injury.

As mother and son stared with wide-eyed amazement at the miracle displayed before them, the bunny, unaware of its enthralled audience, slowly opened its eyes, blinking lazily. Stretching once again, the infant animal slowly got up from his warm sleeping place and seeming to test his balance, hesitated briefly. Apparently assured that all was stable, the fragile creature limped delicately into the trees at the edge of the shaded walkway.

Mother and child stood gazing intently for a long astonished moment in the direction of the retreating junior cottontail. Then without any semblance of warning, the prevailing silence was abruptly interrupted by a crackling sound that seemed to be coming from the same area where the small animal had just vanished.

Reaching out to grasp her child, KayLee pulled back from the weedy overgrown area and started to withdraw to the center of the path. As she tried to step hurriedly away from the rustling sound that was coming closer, perhaps bringing with it the appearance of some threatening animal, KayLee's foot struck the side of a jagged, protruding rock. As she stumbled backward, she felt a tearing sensation on the outside of her right ankle.

Crying out as she fell to the ground, KayLee looked around to see if Samuel was still beside her. He was standing directly above her, looking alternately at her and then turning to look apprehensively in the direction of the approaching rustle. Before either mother or son could react to the new dilemma, a towering male figure came walking out through the thick brush. Neither said a word as the man of mammoth proportions, his shoulder-length auburn hair and autumn-hued beard commanding their undivided attention, moved slowly forward to stand before them. Kneeling down beside KayLee, the modern day

Ulysses, (KayLee's immediate impression) reached a steady hand toward the weakened ankle. The deep, yet somehow calming voice that penetrated the stillness of the surrounding forest was considerate but determined. "If you don't mind, I would like to take a look at that foot."

KayLee's vision became magnetically focused on the fathomless aquamarine eyes of the stranger who was now so close she was certain she could hear the beat of his heart. But she knew in a simultaneous instant that the erratic rhythm that was rocking her senses wasn't coming from this stranger who was but a breath away from her, but rather was escaping from the depths of her own life-giving system. The cadence against her chest was so powerful that its sound penetrated her mind and closed off all the natural songs and strains of the enclosed wooded area. She hadn't felt this kind of reaction since... it had been a very long time. A lifetime ago. It frightened her, even while it captivated her. She should be protesting the intimate touch from this unknown intruder, but for some reason she felt mesmerized. A puzzling thought was whirling through her mind. Why did this person, someone she had never before seen in her life, not seem like a stranger?

Samuel watched, stunned into his own silence as the giant man checked his mother's swollen ankle. A new feeling seemed to be moving in to cover the fear and sadness he had been filled with only minutes ago. Samuel watched as the man's large hands gently pressed around on his mother's ankle and he saw with each inquiring touch, painful creases erupting on his mother's normally stoic expression.

As the stranger briefly straightened his back, Samuel's eyes followed the bearded man's every movement. The boy watched as one long, muscled arm reached into a tan cloth bag that was secured to a thick strap encircling the woodsman's waist. As the man brought out several rolls of white waffle-like cloth, Samuel's mouth dropped open. He wanted to speak, but no words came out as his eyes became fixed on the stranger who was now unrolling the soft, white material and beginning to wrap it around his mother's injured foot.

Samuel watched as if in a trance as each new roll of stretchy ribbon unfolded and was carefully applied to his mother's now moderately swollen leg. The white cloth. Was…was it the same…? It looked just like… Samuel's gaze dropped to the ground. His overcrowded mind was spinning like a top and the questions were whirling around with each rotation, colliding so repeatedly with one another that he couldn't seem to separate them into single thoughts.

When the man from the woods took yet another roll from the small bag, and began crisscrossing the strips around the injured limb, Samuel moved closer to his mother's side. Looking first at his mother's bandaged foot then raising his head to glance toward the path that had led them to their present situation, a sense of deep concentration covered the boy's youthful features. Slowly turning his head so he could once again steer his attention toward the person who had come walking out of the woods to find them just in their time of need, Samuel's cinnamon-colored brows pulled together so tightly they nearly touched at the bridge of his nose. The situation had now reached a point where the young boy's curiosity was getting the best of him. The time had come where silence no longer took priority. The similarity was just too close to hold back one small boy's curiosity.

"Ex-Excuse me, sir, but I... I was wondering..." The question that was roving around in Samuel's mind was proving to be a little more difficult to ask than he had expected, but how else would he find out. He had to try. "By...by any chance are you...are you the one who...uh, did you...?" Samuel suddenly stopped in the middle of his sentence, a hint of hesitancy lingering in the stillness of the surrounding air. Something more intense was overriding his curiosity.

Forgetting about the thought that had been puzzling him, the young boy cleared his throat loudly, pulled his shoulders slightly back, and putting his best display of authority before him, said in a stern, determined manner, "Are you sure you know what you're doing, mister? That's my mother, you know, and I wouldn't want you to hurt her. I'm responsible for her, in case you didn't know."

Straightening his shoulders now to full alert, Samuel stared directly into the glistening sea-green eyes of the kneeling giant. The gruff tone of authority with which the child spoke gave the impression that he was more a protective parent than a young boy, a boy who only moments ago had been completely devastated by the incident on the path. Both adults stared in awe at the lad, struck speechless at the outburst, and each wondered identically how this youngest member of the gathered trio, had so suddenly become very much in charge of the present crisis.

Halting the movement of his hand in midair as he was about to make another under-wrap on the impaired foot, the burly man turned to face Samuel. Seeing the intense concern etched on the youthful features, the man spoke in the quiet reassuring manner he had been accustomed to using those many years ago when consoling anxious family members.

"Yes, young man," (There was that title again. The tightened surface of Samuel's face loosened as he heard the words sent his way for the second time that day.) "I do know what I'm doing. I have done this before... many, many times. I am being most careful. I give you my word; I will not hurt your mother. You see, I used to be...I...I was..." The big man hesitated, glancing briefly to the ground. Then taking a deep breath, he continued. "I...I'm (go ahead Markus Garrity, say it. Say it out loud. Let them hear it. Hear it yourself finally after all these years), "I'm...I'm a doctor. And...and a very good one."

There he had said it. After all these years. And now that he had, Dr. Garrity once again felt a resurgence of the pride and self-confidence that had at one time been such an integral part of his life and career. Had been, that was, until that dark day when all his staple characteristics had disappeared, cast aside by profound sorrow and loss. Shadows had moved in to smother him that somber evening when the light had gone from his life. So long ago and yet only yesterday.

But now... it had felt good. Felt right to say it out loud. But why now? Why in front of these two people? These strangers? A woman and a child he hadn't known until only minutes ago? Admittedly, he still didn't know them, but they didn't seem like strangers for some reason. How could that be?

Taking another deep, cleansing breath and feeling the tension leave his body after so many years of keeping his emotions tightly bottled up, Dr. Markus Garrity looked at Samuel, and with a hint of a smile said to the once again speechless boy, "Now, young man, I would like to ask you a question. Is it all right with you if I finish my job here and try to make your mother as comfortable as possible so I can get both of you and that new bicycle of yours back home? I really should have asked your approval first before helping your mother. That's standard protocol for…(realizing a small child would not understand such a grown-up term, the doctor interrupted his intended explanation and went on in a more simplified manner) …that is… well, let's just say I should have asked your okay before applying this bandage. I hope you will accept my apology. But if you will give me that permission now, I will make this one final wrap and then I'll see that you both get home safely. Do I have it?

While listening for an answer, the doctor glanced briefly at the woman who was waiting to have the procedure completed that this stranger had started when he had first knelt down beside her. Even though the confession he had just made about his professional status must have been somewhat of a shock to the woman he was attending, and the fact that she had to be in at least a moderate state of pain from her injury, the man was taken back momentarily by the serene, delicate features that met his vision. There was a gentle smile, rimmed with beaming pride, related without question to the action just taken by her loving, caring child.

Turning once again to look at the now quieted boy standing behind him, the renewed man of medicine saw his answer.Samuel stood in silence, but nodded his head in approval and then watched with deep fascination as the doctor applied an expert hand one more time to finish wrapping the cloth bandage around the injured leg.

When the ankle wrap was completed to the doctor's professional satisfaction, and to the child's amateur one, Samuel turned away from the first aid scene. He took a few steps and began pacing back and forth through the thick underbrush, clenching his hands repeatedly. KayLee watched her young child, wondering silently why he seemed so uneasy, so perplexed. Something was bothering him; that was obvious.

Samuel turned to face the wooded pathway once again and then slowly pivoted in place to look back directly at the big man who had so abruptly changed from a mysterious monster of the woods to a gentle, helping stranger. Clearing his throat softly, and pulling at the bottom hem of his t-shirt in an anxious twitching manner, Samuel's voice broke through the pervading silence.

"Sir, that is…Doctor, I…I'd just like to tell you that you, ah, you did a…a very good job fixing my mother's foot. So I guess…I guess you are who you say you are. Not that I didn't believe you." Here Samuel paused, shaking his head side to side enthusiastically as proof of his convictions, and then went on. "Because I did, really. Well, almost right away anyway, but you…you have to admit, it isn't every day you meet up with a doctor in the woods, you know. For a minute there I thought you might just be feeding us a line. Like to cover up the fact that you might be some dangerous bank robber or something."

Samuel was so engrossed in his own conversation that he didn't notice his mother and the tall man as they each brought up a hand to cover the smiles that were threatening to break through the seriousness they meant to convey.

"Well, anyway, I was wondering if I could ask you just one more question. There's something I would really like to know." If he had to postpone the question too much longer KayLee was certain the one corner of Samuel's t-shirt would be in shreds. With each word he spoke, Samuel gathered up more and more fabric as the twisting intensified. The child definitely had an important question to ask the newly addressed medicine man.

Forcing an intruding smile to retreat, Markus Garrity's eyes betrayed him as they filled with a tenderness and yearning he could not hold back. Looking down at the little redheaded boy who displayed blue trusting eyes and a congregation of burnt umber freckles, the man listened with undivided attention as the juvenile caretaker's words burst forth without thought or plan.

"Yes, son…?" The word echoed back to him as if a clap of thunder had sounded directly into his ears. Son? Had he really said "son"? It had escaped so easily, so naturally and somehow it…it felt right. Predetermined. "What would…what would you like to know?" The brief hesitation vanished as the man waited to hear the child's request.

"Well, there was this little rabbit who...who somehow, ah, got hurt over there on the path." Samuel stole a quick glance at his mother, hoping to have her approval that he didn't have to explain further. Seeing her sad smile and the slight nodding of her head, he continued on.

"Anyway, when I saw how badly he was hurt, I picked him up very, very carefully and put him over in the soft grass off the path so no one else could come by and accidentally hurt him again. Then I ran as fast as I could to get my mother so we could help him. But when...when we got back to the place where I had hit...uh, where I had put him, he was gone."I felt sooo scared when we couldn't find him. After all, I was the one who had..." Samuel took in an extended breath of air and after exhaling slowly, paused briefly while lowering his glance to the ground. When he lifted his head, he turned once again to face his mother. The reassuring smile that was directed right at him, gave him the courage he needed to finish his request.

Clearing his throat in preparation, Samuel began to speak, his confidence coming back in gradual steps. "As...as I was say...saying...." The boy coughed softly before he went on. "Just...just as we were about to give up on finding him, a miracle happened. A genuine miracle." This last was said with an emphasis of utter amazement, again bringing smiles to the audience in attendance. The joy of the previous discovery now erased the child's hesitancy. His words flowed out with tranquil ease.

"My mother found him sleeping by some fuzzy purple flowers at the side of the path and called me over to look. When the little bunny felt the warmth of his nest being disturbed, he stretched out his legs... well, at least three of them, and the next thing we knew he was going off slowly into the woods. And that was when I saw the white ribbon cloth and what looked just like a Popsicle stick tied to his leg. It was wrapped just...well, um...just the way you wrapped my...my mother's leg, except for the Popsicle stick, of course." Samuel gave a quick, unsure smile, then shrugging his shoulders, continued on. "When you unrolled the cloth for my mother's foot, I couldn't help noticing that the white material looked awfully familiar and that maybe you...ah...that...well, that maybe you...you were the one who had fixed the rabbit too. It was just a guess, but it looked pretty suspicious."

The man's timbering voice released the tension of the boy's camouflaged confession. "That was very observant of you, son." Interpreting the boy's unspoken words, Dr. Garrity felt touched by what he knew was the child's heartfelt, self-imposed penance, and wisely allowed the veiled confession to slide into the past, as he had unknowingly just done with his own episode of self-inflicted guilt. There was no outward sign shown by the man from the woods that he had guessed the details of the unfortunate incident. He simply forged ahead, intent on settling the boy's probing curiosity.

"And I have a feeling you'll be proud to know that you have guessed correctly," he continued. "The rabbit's doctor and your mother's doctor are one and the same. I'm very impressed that you figured that out.

Maybe you should consider being a detective some day."

Samuel's eyes sparkled brightly at the issuance of the compliment, and he instantly wondered if it was possible to be both a pilot and a detective at the same time. But as quickly as the thought came, it retreated. His face once again took on a serious look as he got back to his intended mission. Straightening to his full height, which wasn't much more than the height of the young deer Markus Garrity had rescued recently, Samuel got directly to the point.

"Well, thank you for those good words, sir, but there is something else I've been trying to figure out. After I saw how you fixed up my mother's leg so good, and figured out that it was a pretty sure thing that you were the one who fixed the rabbit's leg, too, there was this stuff twirling around in my head that I just couldn't understand. I mean, to do the magic fixing up that you did today you have to be pretty smart, so it's troubling me that you haven't thought of the idea on your own. I hope I'm not being too snoopy, but, well, this is the question I want to ask you. Since you seem to be such a good leg doctor, wouldn't you like to go back to school and learn how to fix other parts, too? It seems like such a waste of time to just sit around waiting for someone to hurt a leg so you have something to do."

That it might be possible for one simple question to contain a power so forceful that it could transform an entire world, seemed beyond the realm of earthly understanding. But it was, nevertheless, happening. The door to the hidden kingdom was opening, releasing sounds that had been locked away for what surely had been an eternity.

As if controlled by predestined will, Samuel's eyes suddenly closed and were mystically sealed by the magic that was swirling around him. Visions of toy boxes bounced happily to and fro while dancing yellow bears began spilling out as the lids slowly opened. In the world unfolding within his mesmerizing dream, Samuel felt as if his body were floating on air, being transported back to another place, a place that had been so dear to him, and yet so unreachable. He watched as each bear, in unison, opened its mouth and he cheered with delight as the lilting sound erupted, filling the spaces that had too long been void.

At first it started out so softly, Samuel had to strain to hear it. Then it was as if an intricately formed cocoon had suddenly reached its bursting point and with the blare of a thousand trumpets, its binding wrap opened exuberantly, setting free a beautiful new life. A life that at once sent forth sound waves of love and harmony as it dispersed the rainbow colors of happiness. The long absent melody was everywhere.

As Samuel opened his eyes and turned around, he heard the same sound coming from the direction where his mother sat resting on the ground. He heard it erupting from the place where the mysterious man from the woods now stood. It filled the trees. It echoed off the protruding branches. It spread across the path and was carried into the wind, landing everywhere the wafting breezes touched. It had come back so easily. It couldn't have been so far away after all. Perhaps just hiding, waiting for some little boy to discover it, to set it free. And with one innocent question, the sound had returned. The joyous chimes of laughter had at last been found.

Filled to overflowing with his rediscovered joy, Samuel stretched his waiting arms high into the air. Reaching out, he gathered up all those wonderful, precious sounds that were circling throughout his world, and with the trusting, determined grasp of an eager child, he brought them all together in one giant, caressing sweep and pressed them, each and every one, close to his happy, rejoicing heart…making a silent promise to never let them get lost again.

—

As Samuel bathed in his newfound glory, he stopped his splashing about and glanced once again at his mother. He found himself staring at her. There was something very different about her. A glow, a sparkle. Her eyes twinkled like the stars and the smile that had so long been hidden behind a window of sadness broke through, spreading a delightful color of pink across her cheeks. And if he wasn't mistaken, didn't the doctor have the same look about him? Everything was changing right before his eyes. It was just like Christmas morning when the present you opened was the one you had been hoping for all year long. The excitement of it all made him shiver with delight.

Samuel continued to watch the unfolding scene, taking in every act. His attention was fixed now on the doctor. The man brushed aside a few broken branches that were scattered about the ground and then lowered himself to sit down beside his most recent patient.

Time and its somber past seemed to evaporate into the treetops as joyous sounds began to once again fill the air surrounding the little boy. It became apparent that the enchantment of the day had not just been spent on one young child. The two adults sitting under the majestic Christmas tree were, without a doubt, discovering some special magic of their own. The shadows that had briefly crept into the early part of the day were now being chased away by a blazing circle of light. The beams that showered forth promised a happy ending to all who bathed in its glow. Isn't that just how it should be?

—

And they all lived happily ever after.
The lady.
The doctor.
And a laughing, redheaded little boy named Samuel.

THE END*

*THE BEGINNING

EPILOGUE

Once upon a time there was a small boy named Samuel. Samuel lived in a wonderful place that was overflowing with joy and happiness. There didn't seem to be enough time in each day to use all the goodness that filled his life.

If only the future could be seen by those young eyes that looked and saw so much brightness and felt so much love. If it had been possible, if there had been a way, perhaps one would have bundled it all into a basket, put a tight lid on it and hidden it away in a familiar area to be brought out at the time when a great shadow moved in and covered the kingdom with a mist that never seemed to lift.

The cloud appeared to be hiding in every corner of the kingdom. Not only did it shut out the light, but it also covered the sounds, the feelings, everything that made up the very life of the kingdom. The happy sounds of laughter were covered with ease. The strength that had comforted when there was fear…gone. The exciting sounds of a new morning, the gentle tones of the closing day…gone. In a brief wink of time, it was all gone.

Was it a fog so dense that even the sun could not push its golden arrows through it? It couldn't be gone for all time. There had to be a way to bring it back.

And then one day, just when the silence was at its loudest peak, a swirling movement formed high above the darkness. It went round and round until it had gathered such enormous strength that it reached down into the mist and created an opening just broad enough to grab onto the very things that had threatened the small child's kingdom. The dark sadness was drawn upward and filled all parts of the vacuum. With one great whisk of the spiral the once lingering shadow was thrown into space and dispersed into such minute pieces that it would never again be recognized as its old self.

But that was not the only magic that happened that day. With the same velocity that the whirling cloud had descended to rid the kingdom of the mist and quiet, it now made an even wider opening and dropped down myriad rays of sunshine, infinite amounts of laughter, bonding strengths of love.

For so long Samuel had known something was missing from the kingdom, but until he found it, until it was a real part of him, he didn't know what it was that was missing or where it had been. Or even where to look. But now that it had come back to him at last, Samuel knew in all certainty where one had to put all those things that were so precious...a place where they would always be near. There was only one safe place to store all the things that made life so wonderful, so complete. The heart. It was the only place. And once the heart was filled, all the overflowing goodness would spill out to all that surrounded it...and everything that it touched would become a part of that special place known as...Samuel's Kingdom.

virginia rasmussen

"YOU GOTTA PLAY THE MUSIC LOUD"

As I lifted the last of the many cartons that had been sitting on the basement shelves, undisturbed for who knew how many years, I blew a settled layer of dust from its top while placing it on the table next to the ever reliable Maytag washing wonder. I leaned my head over the container and huffed and puffed one more time, reminiscent of the power released by that four-legged creature in Little Red Riding Hood. I became most notably aware that my efforts hadn't made the box fall over, as indeed the house of straw had done, nor to my dismay had any more of the gray particles disappeared. I surmised that the big bad wolf's lungs had not been substantially impaired by polluted basement air, as mine most certainly must be, and were working at full strength the day he performed his dastardly deed.

Accepting this likely deduction, I decided to forgo another pitiful exhalation and instead gave a quick swipe of my hand over the cardboard top. Finding success displayed on my open palm I rubbed my hands together to rid them of the agitating powder and wiped the remains of the adhering residue down the sides of my pant legs. The Maytag would soon have to defend its reputation.

When the air cleared, and I once again was able to return to my normal breathing pattern after coughing and sneezing the pesky residue from my vulnerable sinuses, I looked down at the box I'd been waiting for…the last one! I was surprised and somewhat confused when I saw scrawled across the top of the cardboard container what appeared to be the familiar penmanship of my mother. That is, the writing that *used* to be my mother's. Over the years a wavering hand, that could no longer hold a pen steady as it moved over paper, had affected her perfect script. Okay, I said to myself, I recognize the writing, but where had the box come from?

As the dust continued to settle around me, I felt my nose twitch so I lifted a sleeve-covered arm to give it the honor of catching any forthcoming nasal drip should the inevitable occur. Luckily for my sleeve, I was in a dry spell. I let my stinging eyes recover from the irritating onslaught before I once again turned my attention to the box in front of me. I read the label out loud. I'm not sure why I took to an oral form of reading. It was pretty obvious there was no enthralled audience surrounding me, waiting to be told what only my eyes could see. I was definitely alone in this dungeon whose ceiling was draped with sagging highways of wispy threads (were the spiders actually constructing their own freeway system under my humble abode?). Perhaps it was the surprising discovery of what was displayed before me that caused me to put the words out where I could hear them…as if that would be more convincing than reading them silently.

"Joey's (the name which at some time in the past, had had a thick black line drawn through it and been replaced by the name "Joseph") Elementary Papers, School Ribbons, Yearbooks, and other Valuables." The bold black letters stood out on the old cardboard box as if they had been written yesterday. I felt a twinge of self-chastisement as I glanced once more at the affectionate childhood nickname that had been so broadly, but no doubt wistfully, crossed through. How many times do we regret the stubborn quirks of our youth? After all, the child-like derivative hadn't seemed to bother a grown man such as entertainer Joey Bishop or for that matter, daredevil/stuntman, Joey Chitwood, so why had it…? Regrets? Well, as that life-reflecting song from a few years back dictates, "I've had a few."

As my eyes continued to skim over the letters, I noticed that the flaps of the box had been bound together with strips of scotch tape that had yellowed over the years and were now brittle instead of pliable and adhering. I had brought some durable wrapping tape downstairs with me for resealing any boxes I wanted to keep so I now reached over to the swayback shelf where the box had stood and picked up the roll trimmed with the trademark red, black, and yellow plaid label. (Those Scots really know their adhesives.) My intention was to just pull the separated flaps closer together, slap on a strip of the reinforced tape, and thereby restore the seal on the container of fading school mementos. One of these days I'll probably check them out, I thought nonchalantly, but not right now. My immediate goal was to just get the basement cleaned up and get rid of things that were taking up valuable space. As a matter of fact, I couldn't recall ever looking at any of the old school papers, books, etc., since my school days…more years ago than I cared to think about. Someday when I had more time, I told myself, I would take a quick glance at the sundry items. After all, how interesting could any of that juvenile stuff be?

I hesitated briefly. (Was something telling me not to be so anxious to close the lid on this case yet? No pun intended.) I felt my brow forming small folds as thoughts began swirling around in my head. Where had the box come from? I couldn't remember being so attentive to memorabilia over the last decades that I would have deliberately saved all these bits and pieces from my past. I just wasn't that sentiment...and then it dawned on me. I nodded my head in acknowledgment when I realized that my parents must have brought the box over when they moved out of the home place...the two-story house that had been *my* home, too, for the first twenty years of my life. They had moved into a modest one-story town home about ten years ago. Wanting, but even more so, needing a place where they no longer would have to worry about yard work or dealing with outdoor repairs on their home had made the decision to give up their cherished dwelling somewhat easier than anticipated.

I lifted my hand to pull off a length of tape and was surprised to see that the dispenser was no longer in my grasp. Where...? I glanced down at the table and lo and behold there it lay next to the mysterious box. I couldn't remember setting it down. Apparently I was on a downhill slide over the hills of memory. I shrugged off the confusing thought and just picked up the roll again not wanting to remember how it might have gotten there. Perhaps I should start doing more crossword puzzles. Just last week (or was it the week before?) I had read a newly published report that said doing those aggravating word puzzles was supposed to keep your brain active and aid in alertness as one aged. But it had crossed my mind at the time I was reading that those doggone squares could raise my blood pressure to dangerous heights from the agitation I felt when trying to put the logical word (a seven letter one) into a five letter space. Ward off one infirmity, but set up an invitation for another. Talk about a Catch-22!

Pushing to the background the healthy-living advisory, I pulled out a length of tape and found my hand stopping in midair before tearing the sticky piece off the serrated edge of the roll. "Other Valuables." Hmm. I wonder…Curiosity was moving in on my casual indifference. Well, I guessed it wouldn't hurt to take one quick check on the contents. I was surprised how my heart seemed to pick up a step in pace as I opened the lid and peered inside. So much for not being interested in my past.

The first item that lay at the top of the enduring remnants from my tender years hit my eyes with a flash of pride-filled memory. There, in all its serene lavender glory, was the 3rd place ribbon I had won in a 1st grade "hopping" contest. The rules had stated, as much as I could recollect, that you had to bend one knee and hold on to the attached foot while hopping on your free leg all the way from the rusting monkey bars to the cloud-touching slide.

This well-seasoned, dented wonder, along with its metal-barred companion was a charter member of the recreational trio that formed the Morristown elementary school playground. The other component of this threesome was the set of swings that hung a safe distance from its companions. That was it. The triplets of childhood memories. Oh, but wait a minute. Wasn't there something…? Hmmm. Was there a teeter-totter there, too? And now that I think about it, what was it that had made the playground spin around during our noontime recesses? Seems to me there was some contraption that had chains hanging from it with giant rings at the end of each of those linked arms. If I'm not mistaken I think there were several times I saw my cafeteria lunch again after taking a couple spins on that darn thing. I feel a little light-headed just thinking about it now.

Well, anyway, the other half of the dirt-covered lot was used during phy-ed class. Or as some of you may call it… physical education, P.E., phys ed. How many different labels can one activity have? Nevertheless, to us back then it was phy ed and it was a three-day-a-week class attended by the older boys and girls who made up the remainder of the student body in the three and a half-story red brick building.

The half-story part of the facility came in because the janitor's room and locker rooms were tucked in under the west side of the school just below the main level, and a few steps up from the sunken cafeteria, which at one time had been a gymnasium. The facility held grades one through twelve within its pale green layer-painted walls. Kindergarten hadn't been invented in our small village yet back then.

Back to that all-important contest. I can remember thinking when I was a part of those delicate years and romping around that "giant playground", that the distance between those iodized monkey bars and the sought-after finish line of our various races, seemed to be at least two miles in length. (When I went back to the playground many years later, I can still recall the shock of visual reality that hit me when I glanced alternately at the two pieces of equipment and found to my utter amazement that they were scarcely more than 15 feet apart! The deceptive mirages of youth.)

Third place. That's what I had gotten. I can still see my mother (Dad had to work at the lumber yard so couldn't come to watch my performance) cheering for me as I crossed the finish line and telling me I was absolutely the best little "hopper" she had ever seen. I was never the greatest athlete during my youth, but I guess I hadn't been too bad if I came in third.

As I lay the ribbon down on the tabletop, I let my thoughts ricochet to that day at the races. It was almost as if I were watching a movie screen that was set up in my mind, the film projecting frame by frame, catching even the smallest detail as it went along its spasmodic path.

I could still see all of us all lined up in a row waiting for the whistle that would signal the start of the race. Billy Jensen was standing off to my right, practicing what looked like a dance on a bed of hot coals, alternating feet as he sought his best stance for a sure-fire victory. Jackie Langworthy, on the other side of me, was holding his left leg at a nearly precise 180 degree angle, leaning on my left shoulder to keep his balance checked before we started off; and next to Billy was…ah, next to Jackie was… No. No way. That can't be. But…I mean…how could…? Well, can you beat that? There were only *three* of us, *total,* in that race. And I had come in third!

All those following childhood years I can recall feeling so excited because I had won a ribbon. Me, the plugging turtle in the world of racing. I had bested my own critical predictions. Hadn't I? My mother was so proud of me! She had made me feel as if I were the greatest athlete in the world. I had even gone so far in my self-admiration to think that there weren't even very many rabbits around my neck of the woods that could out-race *me*. How about that. Third out of three. What my mother's attitude had done to *mine*. If the principle she had used that day could have a label put on it in this generation, I believe it would be a proclamation of "positive parenting." She really was something special. Let me rephrase that. Not just *was*, but also still *is*. That's really hard to believe. Only *three* of us?

I picked up the ribbon again, rubbing my fingers over its satiny surface one more time before placing it on top of the Maytag. No reason to put it back in the box just yet. After all, I had hopped pretty impressively to win it. I should keep it out for a little while ...keep it in my field of vision.

Only three of us? I couldn't let it go. I was finding it hard to swallow that penetrating lump of reality. There must have been someone on the other side of Billy. Or at least next to Jackie? Maybe I was just getting a head start on that memory lapse the medical journals were warning about. That certainly was a better explanation than the absence of competition during that most challenging of races. I would have to think seriously about getting a large volume of crossword puzzles. The sooner, the better.

I decided to let that pondering situation dangle a while and directed my attention once again to the open container in front of me. The next item that caught my attention was a business-sized envelope. Pencilled across its front side were the words, "Joey's Hair (and Joseph's Hair!!!!!?) With no less than five exclamation points and a puzzling question mark at the end of the label. Puzzling to *me*, that is. Well, maybe I was going to find out why that punctuation mark had been used. I think I was looking for the solution to the puzzle before all the pieces had been locked together. I turned the envelope over and saw evidence that it had been sealed, opened, sealed again with a coating of glue and then perhaps opened and sealed once again over the years. There were several dried drops of glue dispersed on the envelope's back surface, spilled no doubt during the numerous reapplications.

I slipped my index finger under the crisp flap and as I bent it back to check out the contents inside the folded enclosure, I saw tiny strands of hair stuck to the repeated glued edging. Inside I found two small packets that had been handmade from waxed paper, and upon closer scrutiny noticed that they held several clumps of hair, the second set of strands much darker than the first. Plus there was one other slightly larger waxed folder that looked strangely discolored. Interesting puzzle. (Did this count as much as a crossword challenge? Maybe not since my memory didn't seem to be showing any flashing signs of rejuvenation…no familiarity registering. Apparently the dreaded squares were in my future if bulbs were going to light up any time soon.)

Picking up the waxed folder that held the brown, golden flecked strands, I read its label: "From Joey's first haircut…14 months old." I reacted with a brief smile. Next I took out the folded sheet that contained strands darker and thicker in width than those in the first package. I compared the two colors as I glanced back and forth at the locks that had once been on my tousled top. The second label read: "From Joey's haircut the day before he started first grade…almost six years old. Teacher: Mrs. Zilske." I shook my head from side to side. She had actually saved the clippings. I wondered, as I held the childhood mementos, which one of us had cried the most tears at each of those haircuts. I think I could make a very positive guess.

The third and final enclosure had no note attached. I unwrapped it carefully and out fell, to my surprise and shock, several red, blue, and green strands of… of what? Surely not hair? But it *was* hair. And oh, yes, it was hastily coming back to me. The projector was running again as the screen flashed out before me. I had thought all remnants of that experiment had gone down in one big swirling funnel that long ago day when I had turned that know-it-all age of sixteen.

I had felt obliged to try something really daring with those miniature bottles of food coloring that had been sitting so invitingly on the pantry shelf. Where had she found these rainbow tinted locks? I was certain I had washed away all the tell-tale evidence with one push of that chrome handle, flushing my latest teenage whimsy around, down, and out through the corroding copper pipes to seek refuge under the non-judgmental village streets.

Mothers move in mysterious ways. Isn't it something that she never said anything to me? Or did she? Now that I remember…she did tell me that same evening after supper that my hair seemed to have a special glow and it looked a little shorter in spots than it had that morning. I believe, again if my memory isn't failing me, that I had said something to the effect of combing it a bit differently for a change and I had tried out a new shampoo that had come as a free sample in the mail.

We don't get away with half of what we think we do. Amazing. Hmm. I wonder. Do you suppose Dennis Rodman's hairdresser ever consulted with my mother? I mean, is it possible that I might be the one who originated…? Me? A trendsetter? It's possible.

Speaking of hair. When I think of all the times I was asked, …let me rephrase that,"told" to get a haircut, it might have been a smart move for my dad to make a recording and just play it whenever I walked in the door! I can still hear him. What did I have against a neat trim every now and then? A few days after I had had a haircut, well, okay, so maybe it was more than a few days, but it didn't seem like it back then. The hair on the back of my shaved neck wasn't even soft yet before he started in with his diatribe. "Son, don't you think it's time you go see Charley at the barbershop? You're starting to look more like your cousin Katy every day."

Dad was never subtle about anything. I tried to ignore him, but he made that form of strategy next to impossible. Out of the clear blue sky he'd start his next taunting hint by singing a song that mentioned my cousin's name, said something about her being beautiful and solely adored. When he got to the part about the moon and the mountains, I knew it was time to leave the performance. I would turn and run up the steps to escape the jeering litany, go into my room, close the door and put on my favorite record at its highest volume. The last phrase I heard before the door went shut was something about a kitchen door. Now I ask you, what kind of song was that! The words made no sense.

No way could I cut my hair. Those tresses held magnetic powers. Chicks. The girls loved the way it slicked back and hung over my stand-up collar. I was a "hound dog.' A rebel with a cause. I couldn't take a chance on losing all that in one swift cut of the scissors.

And it could all be lost in one quick swipe of the shears or buzz of the razor. Once you sat down in that barber's chair, you could see the determination in the eyes of the master towering over you that he now had the wherewithal to get the world back into control. Butch haircuts! It made me cringe to even think about it. Adults just lose all concept of that powerful status called "image" in their offspring.

And then there was the music. The lifeblood of our youth. The sounds that flowed freely and effusively through our veins and arteries and kept us more alive than any transfusion could ever have done. Have there ever been parents who have gotten with the times when it comes to tunes? It seems I would just get to my room, get the bop'n rock and roll songs churning, when all of a sudden I would hear a voice at the bottom of the stairway.

"Joey?" Pause. Silence from both parties. It's an unwritten law, of course, one that every teenager knows unconditionally from peer inheritance, that it's standard protocol to never respond to the first holler. They might go away, right? Wrong. No such luck. There it was again. "Joey? Joey, could you turn that Victrola down a little?"

Cringe. "Ma, it's not a *Victrola*. Remember? They went out years ago. I told you, it's a record player. And I can't turn it down. I need it loud."

Silence. Lucky me. I scored again. She went back to the kitchen.

Wrong. Error. Tilt. There it was. The dreaded knock on the door. "Joey?"

Oh man. "Ma, could you not call me Joey anymore? Huh? Pleeease? (Parents. You just can't get through to them.) I'm not in grade school. Remember? I'm almost an adult now. (I'll bet she was surprised to hear *that*!) "Call me Joseph, okay? Okay? You make me sound like a baby. I'm a *teenager*. (A word that, to parents, had to be as dreadful as the word "plague.")

A soft cough. "Joey, I mean… *Joseph*" (said with much more emphasis than the *Joey* was)" I'm going to ask you one more time to turn down that Vic…er, record player and then I'm going to come in there and turn it down myself."

I can, to this day, still visualize her standing there, outside my bedroom door in her faded pink and blue flowered house dress that was starched and ironed to a perfection as if all of her had just rolled out from a steaming mangle press. Her hands were resting on her hips as she tried, oh so hard, to be very stern. Yet there were telltale signs (she just couldn't perfect a sound of genuine anger) that she was not really certain that she would carry through with her threat. And of course, I knew that. Smart aleck teenager that I was.

But then, as always, I would feel myself weaken. After all she was my mother and even if she did have a lot to learn about raising a teenager, I could forgive her these mild shortcomings. But the important thing at hand for this time was that I had to come across with the logic of *why* I couldn't possibly turn the volume down. There are some times when you just have to lay it out on the table (or through the door as this case calls for). Maybe this would convince her. She *had* to see the logic of this one. "But, Ma," I pushed," you gotta play the music loud so you can hear all the parts. You just gotta."

I stayed on my bed and listened for a rebuttal, but none came. I now envisioned her shaking her head from side to side, surrendering to my teenage whims as she walked slowly down the hall to the stairway, her house dress making crispy sounds as flower touched against flower, not even hearing the creak of the worn steps as she descended because the music took care of any other audible signs of habitation in the simple two story house.

A modicum of time passed, for *her* that is, not for *me*. I'm sure confrontation times always come up more quickly for parents. You know, that dreaded 'teenager-approach-time'. Well, anyway, I was on my third or fourth playing of each and every record I owned, while reclining on my pile of pillows and folded laundry. I never could figure out a reason to hang up or put away clean clothes. If I decided to change into a different t-shirt every once in a while I could do it right from the bed. It's all about saving steps.

As I was saying, I thought I heard an extra note between the gyrating beats of my cherished tunes and realized eventually that there was a voice calling me from the bottom of the stairs. It was a tone laced with enduring patience. I estimated it to be much like the calming intonation of a patron saint. Let's face it. All mothers are saints. Who, but a sainted mother could love a teenager?

"Joe… ah…Joseph? Supper is ready. Your dad is home. Would you please come on down?"

I wonder how many times I gave that standard, monotone answer, "I'm not hungry, Ma. I had some cookies after school and I'm full." Sounded good enough to me. She only called once. And she always added, just so I would be reminded of her ritualistic standard, "This is the only time I'm going to call you." It was the only time she *had* to call me. *They* had a plan.

I never moved. Well, let me rephrase that. I didn't move just then. Then it came. Another call. The plan was in action. A different voice. "Joseph Alexander Mikkelson, get your butt down here for supper or I'll come up there and *drag* you off that bed." It's amazing how your appetite comes back when you get a formal invitation.

And, oh, yes, the bed. Another sore spot. My mother couldn't tolerate the sight of an unmade bed. My dad used to say if he didn't get up fast enough each morning, the bed would be made with him in it and the bedspread would be tucked tightly under his chin with no chance of escape. I always thought it was so much more comfortable to just hop in the bed the way you had left it in the morning with all the folds just where you wanted them. That is until I got married and found out that that is just not the way things are done! End of that theory. How do you suppose Einstein proved *his* theory was right?

—

I glanced at my watch as I stood over the box, still holding on to the packets of waxed paper. Where had the time gone? I had covered quite a few years since I first opened the cardboard carton. If I wanted to get to mom and dad's before supper I realized I'd have to get these things back in the box and get going.

As I gathered up the ribbon and the envelope to replace them in the box right next to the yearbooks (those pictorial histories would have to wait for another time), I saw the corner of a sky blue, soft-covered book peaking out from under the crinkled maroon bindings of my high school's annual publications.

As I brought the book out from its near obscurity, I felt my brow crease in puzzlement. I didn't remember ever seeing it before. I turned it over to check if there were any markings on the opposite side or if it was as blank as the portion that faced me. And then it came back to me. Forget the crossword puzzles for the time being. I felt mental recovery stepping to the center of the stage. "A Child's First Journal" was embossed in yellow felt across the top of the cover and holding stance in the lower right corner was a tiny, white fuzzy rabbit.

When I had seen the sky-colored volume for the first time, I was seven years old and it was given to me as a Christmas gift from my dad's Aunt Winnie. Winifred Ernestine Neubauer had been a schoolteacher in a rural area out off old Highway 60 where "all the youngsters had to walk 'miles and miles' every day just to get to school." Hasn't everyone heard that line before? Apparently, *no one* ever lived close to those country schools, which makes me wonder why they were built on their chosen sites in the first place.

"The best teacher you'll ever see," I remembered my dad boasting every chance he got. "That woman knows words that aren't even in the dictionary yet."

At the time I opened the gift, being a very young boy I had no idea what a journal even was. What energy-filled first grader would have wasted precious playing time to keep track of daily experiences at that point? Boys were more interested in *doing* things than *recording* them. But Aunt Winifred (my dad said it was more polite for me to use her given name) was about to explain it very clearly to me as she drew me up and settled me gently across her slender lap (I mentally termed it 'bony' and compared it to the same feeling of sitting on two narrow tree branches.) Once I had stopped wriggling and found a comfortable position, not an easy task given the circumstances of said lap, Aunt Winifred proceeded to inform me in detail about what it was I was holding in my hands.

It was to be my very own book. No one else would have to see it. I was to put things in it that I saw or did as I went about my day. Just ordinary things. Personal "every day" things, she had confided to me, as she lowered her voice so that we would be the only two in on the secretive session. It didn't have to be important worldly events, just thoughts and happenings that little boys were interested in or wished for.

I remembered feeling very special that I was to have my very own book, one that I didn't have to share with anyone else. After thanking Aunt Winnie, (in my excitement I temporarily slipped and used the more informal title which to my relief only made her smile as she winked at my faux pas), I promised I would write every day of my life. I accepted, shyly, her encompassing hug, which once again made me feel as if a tall spindly tree was folding me into its branching embrace. I then tucked the book under my arm and went off in a corner by myself to make what I knew would absolutely and positively be only the first of a zillion million notes I would be writing in the exciting years ahead. I opened the book now to its first page and read aloud the primary entry:

"A B C 1 2 3"

Beneath the slanted letters and dangling numbers I then had proudly written my name…"Joey". It was a solitary entry. The first and only entry to ever reach the yellowed pages of the treasured gift.

But it was a wonderful gift. And even though its pages were blank, I felt as if I just now, this very afternoon, had filled all those other pages with the memories of my youth as I stood alone, down in the secluded basement, with my box of memories.

As I wrapped the tape tightly across the two flaps, once again securing a seal, albeit a temporary one (of that I was certain) on the memories my mother had so lovingly packed away for me, I felt myself wanting desperately to get to my parents' home.

I left a note for Christine, telling her where I was going and that I would stop at one of the fast food places and pick up something for supper on my way home. We'd eat healthier tomorrow.

As I approached the door to my parents' townhouse, I could hear uncustomarily loud music coming from inside. I knocked on the door. When no one answered after the second knock, I took out the key I always kept with me and let myself in. As I walked into the entry hall, I saw through the archway leading to the living room, both of my parents sitting on the sofa together, hand in hand. A Lawrence Welk re-run was on TV and the orchestra (or was it called a band?) was playing what had to be the most energetic polka ever scored.

I stood and watched for several minutes as mom and dad kept time with their feet on the plush powder blue carpet. My attention drifted as I watched my dad. I noticed that he really could use a haircut. There were some long wisps sticking out above his ears. I'd have to give Chuck a call and set up an appointment in the next couple days. It seemed to me that he had just had a haircut, but then time does slip by.

And my mother's hair. While it looked as if she had just come back from Selma's Pin Curl Parlor what with the tight display of waves covering her head, I couldn't help but notice the color. Was the lighting in the living room casting rainbow shadows against those strands or did her hair actually have a purplish pink tint to it?

The music played on. They didn't miss a beat.

As the last jumping note sounded, I listened to the trademark voice. "Thank you, thank you, ladies and gentlemen. That was a won-derful, won-derful display. Now, we'll be right back after a word from our sponsor. We have something verr-ry special coming up for you when we return. We'll all be honored to listen to a won-derful chorus featuring our own beautiful

Norma Zimmer as she sings her version of 'Let Me Call You Sweetheart.' Don't go away."

I saw my parents look at each other and smile. As dad leaned over to kiss mother on the cheek, he saw me standing in the doorway.

"Well, look who's here, Mama. It's our Joseph." As he said the words, he tried getting up from his sitting position, but I motioned for him to stay seated. Mom reached out her hand toward me and said, "Oh, Joey it's so good to see you. Come sit by your mama." Patting the cushion beside her, she smiled as if she hadn't seen me for years instead of just last evening.

I took off my jacket and hung it over a dining room chair, glancing briefly at the table with its chairs left pushed back as if their occupants had just finished supper and hurried away without clearing any of the dishes. But as I studied the display closer, I noticed the only serving dish on the table was a plate that held one cookie surrounded by bits and pieces of crumbs. A quart container of milk stood guard over the sparse setting. I scratched my forehead. It felt like corrugated cardboard.

As I turned around to walk toward the arched opening that led to the living room, I noticed that the bedroom door at the end of the hall was partially open. I found it hard to believe what my eyes were observing. The pillows were not at their usual places, but rather were precariously dangling over the side of the bed. The handmade quilt hung haphazardly down as its peaked corners rested comfortably on the carpeted floor. There were slippers placed at undisciplined angles and it looked as if nightclothes were scattered forlornly at the foot of the bed.

I made my way to the sofa and sat down beside mama. I reached for her hand and asked her how she was doing. With the look of a child who had just opened a wonderfully exciting Christmas gift, she squeezed my hand and chimed exuberantly, "I'm just fine, Joey, just fine. And so is your daddy."

"So have…have you had your supper or am I keeping you from it?" I asked the question with some trepidation, not sure I wanted to hear the answer.

"Oh, we've eaten," she spoke nonchalantly. "We weren't very hungry, though, so we just had some cookies. They were some of those that Christine brought over the other day. Remember? Be sure you have one before you leave, Joey. They're so good and really filling."

As soon as the words hit my ears, I felt my head convulse as if jolted by an electric shock. Wait a minute here. That statement sounded just a little too familiar. I began to feel a trickle of discomfort. Needless to say it didn't take me long to figure out where and when and who had used that excuse before. Was that a twinkle in my mother's eyes or was guilt just toying with my imagination? I didn't want to think about it.

As my mother finished her sentence, my father raised an index finger to his lips and said, "Shhh. Quiet now you two, the show's coming back on. Wait until you hear Norma, son. Now that's a voice that could teach the angels. This is your mother's and my favorite song. Isn't it, dear?" he said, as he looked into my mother's eyes with a love that could only come from years of companionship and caring.

I watched my mother nod her head and saw tears form in both my parents' eyes as the old tune echoed throughout the room. My eyes became misty, too, as I watched them, but the mood was soon lost as the music began to trounce on me from all angles. The volume was so loud my ears felt as if they were vibrating.

I got up from the sofa, releasing the hold on my mother's slightly trembling hand, and walked toward the television set to lower the volume to a more tolerable level. As I reached for the dial, my movement was halted abruptly as my father's words leaped out harshly from behind my back *"What* are you doing, Joseph? Stop right there." And my mother, at the same time jumped at me with a tone I had never heard even during my most obnoxious teenage years.

"Joey, what are you *doing*?" I felt like a trampoline. They were verbally bouncing on me from every direction. I think those two could have stopped Humpty Dumpty in midair.

I turned around, facing the two of them, and said in a matter-of-fact voice, trying to hide my shock from their forceful attack, "Oh, I'm… just turning the sound down a little. It's… pretty loud." I nodded my head and crinkled up my face as if to prove the fact.

My father looked at me as if I had lost all my senses and reiterated in a tone that would accept no rebuttal, "Well, son, you can't do *that*. Now you just come back over here and leave those buttons alone. I don't know about you young people. You'd think you could've figured that one out on your own. I'm surprised at you, Joseph. Don't you know…you 'gotta play the music loud or you can't hear all the parts?'"

As the two very special people in my life focused their attention once again on the din coming out of the vintage mahogany console, I returned, chastised, to my place on the sofa. Leaning back into the cushions, I listened as the timeless love song blared out its pleas and declarations…the finale erupting to fill every corner of the encircling room.

I nodded my head knowingly as the realization hit home.

Touché. *

* 13 Across: __ __ __ __ __ __

A six-letter word meaning "What goes around comes around"

THE THREE OF HEARTS

There was no need to glance at the old wooden school clock that hung stoically on the parlor wall to verify what time it was. Angela Wellerman was in the company of a trusty human timepiece that religiously issued that announcement each morning at the first light of day. In a matter of seconds, if they hadn't already formed their vertical position, the bold black hands on the vintage clock would be posing at strict attention for their first six o'clock stance of the new day.

He never wavered from his set routine. His daily emergence was as calculated as that of the rising sun. As a matter of fact, the two events were perfectly in sync. The thumping sound of the ball as it hit the scarred boards of the dilapidated garage, echoed hesitantly in the weight of the dense early morning air.

Side-stepping a burnished copper umbrella stand, the retired school principal reached out to lift one of the louvered slats covering the narrow parlor window. As she peered through the marginal opening, a feeling of espionage and, admittedly, human weakness juggled with her conscience. Willpower was a strength she had acquired over the years in order to remain in control of the lifestyle she had chosen for herself those many years ago. And she was in control for all outside appearances. But the emptiness that she suffered inside volleyed recklessly on the surface of her heart sending shock waves of remembrance as each pulsating beat reached its peak. These emotional actions were a constant reminder of the precious gift of life she had opted to release that one early spring morning a lifetime ago.

Pushing the past aside, as Angela had become accustomed to doing in order to hold fast to the gifts of the present, she felt a need to chastise herself for the actions she was displaying at the moment. This weakness she was encountering now was putting a dull finish on her pride. She, above all, knew the value of a person's right to privacy. Hadn't that been the creed she had relished all her life? Yet, and she couldn't deny it, she was spying. It certainly wasn't one of her normal traits. Intruding. Prying. She had to face the facts. None of the behaviors she was displaying now could have the adjective "admirable" hinged to it. Unwittingly, her attention was being drawn to the lot across from the bungalow she now called home.

Her point of focus was aimed at the activities of a young man occupying the graveled area in front of one severely worn-out structure. If her thoughts had been directed to the condition of the aged building, the lady should have wondered how the ancient walls were able to remain in an upright position with even the slightest of outside battering. The crumbling foundation didn't offer much assurance for its survival. But her mind was not set on the dwelling that for decades had housed the Wellerman family vehicles. Instead, she saw nothing except the person who was now adding some zest to those somber, decaying surroundings.

Studying the young man's movements as he challenged himself throughout his routines, the former tennis instructor (a career she had successfully combined with her administrative position) found herself taking mental notes while evaluating the teenager's performance. She could spot natural talent with her eyes closed. The rhythm of the bouncing ball told all. The boy was good. Very good. His mental perception was nothing if not amazing. There was precise, synchronized movement between his retreating step and the thrusting return. The two were as one.

The entranced observer stood at the window unaware that she hadn't taken a meaningful breath for a full sixty seconds. Her natural breathing pattern had been put on hold. His actions seemed to hypnotize her. There was a predisposed pattern evolving before her eyes, one she would have recognized if she had allowed herself to do so. But because of the excitement of watching such unleashed talent, her mind was evading the obvious. Not until a later time would she see a correlation, a familiarity in his actions. But even then something would hold her back from pinpointing its exact source.

—

It had only been four days since she had returned to her hometown, the town where many years ago the carefree days of her youth had disappeared overnight. But reflections of the past were far from her mind these past several mornings as she had stood mesmerized at her window. And her thoughts at this precise moment were occupied with brushing aside any guilt feelings of espionage as she lifted up yet another slat to get a better view.

As she regarded him on this day, the athletic mentor started to feel a bit uneasy with some of the young player's actions. It was almost as if she could predict his next move. For some inexplicable reason she didn't want to find even the slightest hint of error in his performance. She certainly didn't expect his play to be flawless. Not for a minute. In her many years of training and instructing, perfection was not an expectation. Not in her students, not in her educators, not in herself. Discipline, yes, but never perfection. Yet, there was something about this young man that made her want him to excel above all others. She felt a sudden roiling in the pit of her stomach. Was it because there was something that reminded her of … She shouldn't go there. She really shouldn't. It was too painful. Over the years she had visualized his face among her students. Looked for similar traits… Would his eyes have been brown like hers or would they have been…Stop it, she reprimanded herself. This was crazy. The young man she was observing was a stranger and like it or not she had most definitely acquired the label of a snoopy old busybody. It was time she took hold of the situation by getting away from the window and returning to the task of unpacking the two boxes she had set aside the other morning when she had first been distracted by the familiar sound of a bouncing ball.

"Angela Wellerman," she admonished herself, using her full name for stricter effect, "step back. You're only an observer. You retired, remember?" But in her mind she knew that even though she had physically retired from her position as a mentor, the keen insight, the natural critiquing capabilities, the abiding interest …these facets of her character would never draw a pension. They would stay active and alert for the rest of her days.

—

After apparently hitting a warped board, the bouncing ball deflected at an undisciplined angle to the far left side of the solo player. The engrossed observer found herself mentally responding with the solution to the situation.

It was the first return he had missed. How she had wanted to shout out to him. She could see the move he had to make. Too late he must have realized what was needed to connect with the meandering ball, for he had overcompensated for his error and nearly fallen to the pebble-covered surface. Angela watched with amusement as the player tapped the side of his head with an index finger as if reminding himself to think. His own disciplinarian. The former instructor smiled, unaware that she was doing so, and at the same time began thinking out loud, moving her lips but emitting only a whispered sound.

"Very commendable. I like to see a pupil who recognizes his mistakes and then tries to prevent them from happening again." Which was proven on the very next play when the ball took the exact wayward hop, but this time the player met it hard and "took it home."

Watching as the slender, but muscular arm raised the racquet to hit the felt-covered globe again and again, Angela's trained eye gave her pause to make a more in-depth critique. "He has good movement. A natural rhythm. Very much like…" Shaking her head, to ward off the self-imposed frown, the former tennis instructor once again brushed aside the comparison. "As a matter of fact, excellent pace perception," she murmured, forgetting her former thought, and went on as if explaining his talents to an inquiring recruiter. "His ability to anticipate the flow of motion is a natural gift. He will be a challenger to compete with the best. His is a talent not seen every day and you can mark my word, wherever he plays, the spotlight will be directed at him."

As she continued her observation, Angela once more became silent, her mind assessing the action as it unfolded. There was something else then that started chiseling away at her. He was near perfection on his solo play as far as reading his own moves, which isn't always as easy as one might think, but if he were up against an opponent…

As her scrutiny continued, Angela began to pick up on a gesture that she foresaw could ultimately affect the outcome of an intense contest. There was, at times, an intimation given by the player that enabled the former coach to predict what the next move was going to be. A signal to the opposition. But what had it been? As she watched, she concentrated on each of the slams trying to discover the indicator. There. There it was. Not an all-out hint, but one that could most certainly be picked up on, if not by the opposing player himself then by a perceptive sideline coach. It occurred just before that charging, perhaps winning, return. An acute jutting motion of the left elbow. It was brief, a mere wink of a movement, but it was there nevertheless.

Angela continued to focus on the solo performer, intensely absorbed. Nodding her head when it happened again, she inwardly felt self-pleasure that her observation skills remained so precisely honed. "No doubt about it," she confirmed aloud. Nine times out of ten it would probably go unnoticed to a contesting novice, she surmised mentally, but to the die-hard competitor, one who watched for even the slightest prediction of a move, it could be the tell-tale sign that would steal the winner's trophy right from under a player's jutting elbow!

Unable to restrain herself any longer, Angela let the metal slats fall back into their normal positions. Turning away from her elusive vantage point, she reached over to grab a red windbreaker that was offered to her from an extended arm of the coat stand that stood at attention in its corner post. Throwing the jacket haphazardly around her shoulders, she pressed the release button on the brass door latch. Opening the solid oak door with an ease not generally accomplished against its heavy weight, the athletically toned professional stepped out into the early morning light of the new day. As the warm damp air enfolded her, she realized there was no need for a wrap and nonchalantly pushed it off her shoulders, allowing it to fall heedlessly to the cemented walkway.

For a woman who was orderly beyond a fault, rigidly controlled in all she did, this casual discard gave further proof that she, Angela Wellerman, had a genuine task formulating in her mind. She was on a mission. A compelling drive was overtaking her disciplined willpower to not get involved. It had pushed her out the door and across the way to offer positive criticism to someone who, and she didn't doubt it for even one minute now, was destined to become a champion on the courts.

As the spirited woman stepped briskly over the dew-covered lawn to cross the graveled road, so engrossed was she in her pursuit to meet the young man on the other side, that she was totally unaware that she was still wearing her terrycloth slippers. As soon as she felt the sharp pebbles pressing into the ill-protected soles of her feet, she realized how shoddy her footwear was under the present conditions and this simultaneously reminded her of the visit she had made just the day before to the mayor's office.

—

Angela had gone to city hall to check out the reason her acreage was not fronted with asphalt, while it seemed the standard for all the other village streets. The vicinity's latest returnee was told that the property adjacent to hers was directly on the city limits line, so therefore, when the city street department paved the road they stopped at the recorded boundary line and her frontage remained gravel-coated.

Well, so much for that. There was a small consolation though. The Wellerman bungalow was the last dwelling on the dead end street that led directly into the Southland Woods, and because of that, there was no through traffic to raise the ensuing dust. For that much, at least, she was grateful.

In spite of the aggravating stones, the discomfort she felt was only short-lived. The lady had more important things to think about than the condition of her feet. Her mind was set on the individual hitting intensely at a bouncing yellow ball, and her every thought was directed toward that scene. As the woman's steps quickened, a rabbit, intending to cross the road from near the antiquated garage, saw the galloping figure as it approached his pathway and abruptly changed his route, scuttling back across the narrow boulevard from where he had originated his anticipated journey. He quickly found a loyal haven under one profusely decorated bush whose lavender ornaments had only recently lost their sweet youthful fragrance and were now relegated to stoically displaying the shrunken purple remnants of their old age.

For some obscure reason, but one instinctively known to the four-legged creature seeking shelter, the leaping round object that was making all sorts of commotion next to his nesting place, didn't seem to be as profound a threat to his well-being as did the rapidly approaching figure. There was a veil of staunch determination covering the face of the human entering his animal domain and it seemed to project a warning beam that called for immediate flight from the bordering territory. On second glance, the swiftly moving lady did perhaps look harmless enough, but…best not to push fate.

The draping bush, although not wearing its most becoming costume, did, nevertheless, still have a cloak of appeal. Even in its lackluster state, it stood justly proud and most honorable as it offered one very reputable hideout for one desperately scrambling rabbit. Without a tall black hat or a magic wand in sight, the furry creature disappeared, the density of the bush providing the mystique of the moment. And once again the sure-footed burrower was reminded of his omniscient mother's prophetic creed of wisdom: "Seek

119

ye not foolishly a refuge of crowning perfection, but rather grasp wisely and briskly at one that is laden with opportunistic availability." In other words, "When opportunity knocks…"

—

As the most recent newcomer to the village of Blooming Grove stepped across the jagged pieces of cement that had at one time been a substantial walkway, the modern day descendent of the family whose property she was now approaching, paused momentarily to wait for a break in the vigorous action. When none came after several minutes of silent regard, her presence seeming to be totally nonexistent to the engrossed performer, Angela coughed voluntarily to draw attention. She disliked the fact that she was interrupting a practice routine, but she couldn't hold back her enthusiasm any longer. Direct action was called for. She loudly cleared her throat when the cough didn't register her appearance, and more hastily than intended, snappily approached the graveled drive.

With the next connection of ball and racquet, the dust-coated ball made a peripheral landing and bounced against the woman's leg as she reached the loosely packed dirt surface. Bending down she retrieved the rolling ball and scooped it into her hand. As she looked toward the area where the ball had started its wayward journey, she heard a startled gasp and was immediately lavished with apologies from the young adult male who appeared to be overly distraught for such a minor infraction.

"Oh, I'm so sorry, Ma'am. Are you all right? I should be watching what I'm...I...I thought I heard something and I turned my head just as the... Did the ball hit you? I...I'm...

The concerned look on the young man's face gave cause for Angela to offer verbal assurance that she would most certainly recover from the minor incident. And while she considered it even less than minor, the expression on the face of the young man across from her seemed to portray a different image. He looked as if he had inflicted a wound of major proportions.

"Of course, I'm all right," she offered. "I'm fine. It's only a tennis ball, you know, and it certainly isn't the first time one has put its mark on me." Her voice relinquished a matter-of-fact tone as she spoke her first words to the youth, and then as she continued, reversed roles and presented an entreaty of her own. "But the truth of the matter is, *I'm* the one who should be apologizing for interrupting *you*. It's just that I heard this strange sound, like...like someone pounding or ..." ('Oh, that's good, Angela,' her conscience seemed to be needling her with that latest retort. 'As if this is the first morning you've heard it! And, besides, you could recognize the sound of a bouncing tennis ball with plugs in your ears! When has evasiveness ever been your strong point? Admit it. You're a snoopy old woman.')

Now the boy looked even more contrite. "Oh, no, did I wake you up? I'm really...I'm so sorry. But I...I didn't ...I didn't know anyone lived across from this old...this place. It looks so deserted down at this end of town, I didn't think I would be disturbing anyone. I'll just pick up my things here and be on my way."

121

As he bent over to pick up the blue jacket that lay on the grass next to the neglected cement pathway, Angela interrupted his dismissal by perking up haughtily and with hands on hips, exclaimed, "And where do you think you're going young man? You'll never perfect that forehand hit of yours if you only practice a few minutes each day. You haven't even worked up a good sweat yet."

A startled look came over the teenager's face as he stared in astonishment, his mouth dropping open, at the prim lady who was now nearly standing in his shadow. As he peered into her face, he watched the woman's guise change from one of stern accusation to one that mirrored soft, polite consideration. And if he wasn't mistaken, he thought her tongue was pushing against the inside of her cheek and she was about to break out with a wide, enveloping smile. Which is exactly what she did while offering him her hand.

"Good morning, young man. My name is Miss...ah...Angela Wellerman" Reaching out she grasped his hand and shook it gently but yet with a clench that bespoke firmness. As the strong feminine hand met with his, the youth was temporarily stunned into silence. He paused hesitantly, not moving his hand. Unable to move it. A strange sensation sent shivers up his arm. There was a touch of familiarity. It was... He felt the creases on his forehead pull together as they formed pondering folds. It was strange, puzzling, but, it...it... A bonding grip. But how could that be? He'd never seen this woman before in his life. For a dashing second there was a simultaneous reaction from the joined hand. Odd...most odd. Had she felt it too?

Shaking her head as if a supernatural force had just jarred it, Angela quashed the perplexing intrusion and continued her introductory conversation without letting the young athlete get in a further word. She needed to ward off whatever mutual interaction had just taken place. A feeling of discomfiture was threatening to complicate the naturalness of the situation. It was up to her to take charge and do it quickly. A talented young man was standing before her and she was here to offer her assistance. And that was the whole of it.

Much to her surprise, for she certainly didn't feel composed, she heard herself speak in a light, controlled tone. "Soothing" was an even more accurate description of her voice. How had she managed the metamorphosis so abruptly and completely? She amazed herself with her accomplishment. While her calm facade exhibited control, turmoil still roiled deep within her. The discipline training of all these past years was being tested. It was definitely a fact that when a situation hit a more personal target, it became a greater challenger.

"Now you just calm down, young man," Angela began. "First of all, as I said, the ball left no damage on this well-seasoned exterior of mine. Secondly, you most certainly didn't awaken me; you'd have to be here long before the sun comes up to do that. And third, this place *was* deserted until four days ago when I moved in across the street. So you see, you are hereby pronounced completely innocent of any intrusion on my personal well-being and the assumption that you had been alone at this end of the lane was absolutely correct until, well, as I said, until just a few days ago."

The reassuring smile that the lady exhibited after her short dissertation brought a prolonged sigh of relief from the young adult who stood before her. She took further note at the conclusion of her offered reprieve that his shoulders, reactively being held at fixed alert, now settled into a more natural, relaxed position. At the same time, Angela became acutely aware of her own return to mental and physical tranquility.

Delving into his mental dictionary for words, the teenager had difficulty locating the proper ones. He stammered with several choices before finally coming up with what still sounded more or less apologetic, but had the quality that made one realize he wasn't quite certain of the reason for said apology. "Well, I'm…I'm sorry if I have done any…anything wrong, that is, if you'll just tell me what I've done, I promise not to let it happen again." Looking questionably at the woman who remained standing near him, he saw no hint forthcoming of why she had approached him. And then his face took on a look of dawning acknowledgment. Wires seemed to be connecting to spark his inert state of awareness. The old, visibly deserted lot. That must be it. Now he'd done it. He was trespassing. Way to go, Gabriel.

—

The very minute that Gabriel had unpacked the container holding his duffel bag of tennis equipment, he had set out in search of a place to practice his moves. Discovering that there were no public courts in the village, he started a trek that took him to various sections of town searching for any area that might accommodate his training. Late in the afternoon as he was about to give up hope of finding anything, he had come upon this disheveled lot, a place that looked as if it had been neglected for years on end. There hadn't seemed to be anyone around this far end of the neighborhood (he had knocked several times on the door of the yellow house across the street) when he had discovered the spot two weeks ago, just hours after he had arrived in Blooming Grove with his parents. His family had traded a life style of traffic jams, toll roads, frenzied shoppers, overcrowded suburbs, all of it, to take up residence in this tranquil village they now called home.

Not that there hadn't been adjustments to make with that transformation. Everything new had its challenges. But as a family they had decided that the hectic pace associated with big city living was not how they wanted to live, and besides, his father wanted to be closer to the area where he…well, it just seemed as if the move was predestined. After all the research his father had done, an invisible arrow seemed to point in the direction of this small midwestern town. There was the chance that he might uncover only a route taken, not the final destination, but even that minute finding might hold a beam of light that could penetrate some of the shadows that clouded his father's unknown past.

"I'm on your property, aren't I." It wasn't a question, but rather a derived statement. The youth surmised this deduction as he stood facing the woman, but now seeing her expression he wasn't so sure he was assuming correctly. She didn't really appear to be all that upset. Maybe they didn't deal with first offenders too harshly in small towns such as Blooming

Grove. Mentally he was still living under the regulations of big city laws as he warily weighed the consequences of his present situation.

As a trickling hint of laughter touched the humid morning air, Gabriel Phillips released the breath he had been holding in anticipation of the reprimand he was certain would be forthcoming from the fitfully trim lady standing before him. But upon hearing the surprising response, he took a chance at feeling cautiously optimistic that he wouldn't be spending the afternoon at the local sheriff's office, which consisted of one card table and two wooden folding chairs that were placed incongruously in a back corner of the local fire station, the more wobbly of the two paint-spattered chairs no doubt being the one used for the alleged offender during questioning. There would be no comfortable seating for a wrongdoer in this town!

Angela's eyebrows arched, forming rigid pleats across her forehead while her eyes twinkled in direct response to the absurd prospect that anyone would even consider a trespassing violation when they were on her unkempt abandoned lot. But when she saw the anxious look that remained on the young man's face, she pushed her proposed retort aside, offering instead an assurance that trespassing wasn't even in the dictionary as far as her aging property was concerned.

"Young man, while the property you are standing on is indeed mine, I can tell you in all certainty that I do not consider it an intrusion in any way, form or matter, much less labeling it trespassing. If you have chosen this spot to do your practicing, I consider it an honor to have you do so. I'm afraid, though, that the amenities of such an orphaned lot are few and far between. And besides, you have given me several days of pure joy just watching you perform. ("Now that wasn't so hard to admit after all, was it," Angela silently convinced herself, as she emitted an audible sigh of surprised relief before continuing). "I didn't come over here to chase you away, I came over to offer you a few pointers."

At the issuance of those words, Angela saw the boy's mouth drop open yet another time, and noticed his dark eyebrows jut inquisitively upward as she surmised he was no doubt thinking that he was being visited by some senile member of an undocumented species who, in her acquired dotage, had nothing else to do but look out her window and watch the grass grow. Pulling that summation out to the forefront, the woman smiled brightly and gave a healthy chuckle as she watched the perplexed expression on the young man's face transpose to one deluged with curiosity.

"Ex-excuse me," he stammered questionably, "but did…did you say "pointers?" What… that is…well, what do you know about…? I mean…how would someone your age…?" This wasn't coming out the way he intended. Gabriel let the sentences dangle, warding off the prospect of diving into an even deeper pool of trouble. Best to leave the "age" thing alone. Prudent words donated to him by his mother.

Angela's smile remained in place as she listened to the young man as he tried to figure out his appropriate line of inquiring conversation. She decided it was up to her to throw out a life preserver, once again coming to his rescue. The youthful face was blushing to a feverish shade of crimson as Gabriel weighed out his impending dilemma.

"Let me put it this way…ah…?" pausing briefly, Angela looked questionably at the teenager.

Grasping instantly the meaning of the woman's facial expression, Gabriel automatically started to extend his hand, but instead of clasping onto hers a second time, brought his right palm over and placed it around his left elbow.

"Oh, I'm sorry. I should have… My…my name is… it's Gabriel. Gabriel Phillips." The memory of that first handshake had genuinely perplexed him and with everything else that was happening at this moment in time, he wasn't certain that retesting the previous reaction was in his best interest. The discomfiture remained. Because of his own impending thoughts, Gabriel was unaware that when his hand had gone forward there had also been a brief forward movement and then a subtle withdrawal of the hand belonging to the person directly across from him. Reaction mirrored reaction.

"Well, Mr. Gabriel Phillips," Angela began, replying to the introduction after taking a settling breath, "I'm very pleased to meet you, and as I had started to say, let me assure you that even if I do appear to be ancient and perhaps "over-the-hill" in your eyes,"… Noticing a dawning grimace on the young man's face, Angela paused briefly to issue a tongue-in-cheek smile. She did not halt her litany of explanation, though, but rather continued to draw it out so as not to cause any further disconcerting reaction from the youth she most fervently hoped would be her future pupil.

The desire to teach, to instruct, to offer constructive criticism was a force growing more

128

intense for Angela with each passing minute. What had made her think she could ever get away from it all? Completely detached, anyway. It was as much a part of her as breathing and sleeping. While she, of course, preferred not to give up the former, there were many times over the years when she had willingly given up the latter and would do so over and over again just to see the expression on the face of a student who, after many hours of grueling instructive practice, would finally connect all the moves and elicit a perfectly executed backhand return that had mentally been deemed unattainable.

For Angela it was a personal crown of satisfaction to behold the harvesting of rewards earned by true desire and unwavering dedication. She had spent her entire adult life using her natural skills to help others make their dreams come true and had felt the same depth of joy the participant did when the hours spent at the net delivered positive results. And she was certain beyond all certainty that the young man facing her now was going to be the recipient of one such dream. Never had she been more assured. Gabriel Phillips' destiny was not only being formed by the precise movements of his talented hands, but rather more so within the boundaries of his heart. She saw it. She felt it. It was there, hovering at the surface, just waiting to burst free.

As Angela gazed at the youth standing before her, not only did she see a future for him that held moments of staggering excitement and promise, but looking ahead at her own future she could saw an awakening and rejuvenation of the very joys that had sparked her life all these many years. She felt emotionally and physically regenerated. Retirement? What was that?

Certainly not a word to be found in her existing vocabulary! Life was meant to be lived. One could chose activity or passivity and for right now her choice was being made. There would be no mold growing underneath her shoes (or slippers, for that matter). She didn't intend to be immobile long enough for anything to become attached to them. Age was just a three-letter word that seemed to be taking a detour around one Angela Francine Wellerman.

"What I'm trying to say, young Mr. Gabriel Phillips," she continued as she put her hands into the pockets of her navy blue jogging pants, "I just happen to know a little bit about this game you are playing over here, and I'd like to share some of that knowledge with you, if you'd be so kind as to allow me to do that."

"You know... something about tennis? I mean, how does someone like you...?" Foot in mouth again, Gabriel realized as his face reddened yet another time. Best to listen for a minute and see what this lady had to say.

Pretending as if she hadn't heard the lingering skepticism, his inference to her questionable knowledge of the game in which he obviously was so engrossed, Angela quickly covered his words with her own. "Now if you'll just step back over by that rickety pile of boards formerly known as a garage, I'd like to show you a few moves that will make this whole game a lot more interesting for you and at the same time quite bamboozling for the unsuspecting opponents who will be sharing a net with you."

Angela chuckled to herself as she walked past the stunned teenager and headed in the direction of the wooden relic that only minutes ago had served as an adversary to the energized athlete. There was no visible resemblance of the former youth in the one who now stood motionless as if glued to the sparsely graveled surface. If he looked any more like a statue, Angela feared someone might come along, put him in the back of a truck and haul him off to the park at the east end of town, where he would become a formidable target for the native pigeons!

Reaching the area in front of the garage, Angela halted her steps to take note of the structure's sliding door that hung most decidedly off-kilter. The top plank of the warped portal seemed to be clutching at the loosely attached rusty hinges as if its very life depended on the mercy of these fragile metal anchors. Indeed they were the only lifelines the withering shed had for its rescue. But they too were running out of saving grace, for each had the misfortune of being held fast by just a solitary screw that looked near to giving up the challenge. Shaking her head as she realized the dwindling feasibility of the situation…no way would that door hold up with the onslaught of pounding she had in mind… the energized instructor therefore continued her journey, going around the corner to the side of the building.

Standing yet in the exact spot he had been when Angela Wellerman had begun her trek toward the run-down pile of clinging boards, Gabriel couldn't seem to get his feet to travel in the direction of the swiftly moving woman. Remaining nearly entranced at the situation that had unfolded in the past few minutes, the youth waited in stunned anticipation for what was going to happen next. The morning was definitely taking on a new horizon. All he had wanted to do as the day dawned anew was have his usual quiet hour of hitting, and then, presto chango, into that scene walks an old…ah…a woman who starts talking to him about a game that…well…was really intended for the young and agile. Wasn't it? And now she tells him to go back to where he was and she would give him some pointers! Just the mere thought of that prospect left him shaking his head in puzzlement and wondering what kind of people he was now surrounded by in his new home.

Suddenly the quiet morning air was interrupted by sounds of clanging metal and thumping noises as objects of some sort or other were being thrown against the inside surfaces of the rotting boards. Gabriel could hear sounds of muffled, fragmented words squeezing their way out from within the boundaries of the old structure.

"… know you're in …somewhere around… maybe back… that corner?" More banging of metal against metal, clinking vibrations as sundry items obviously were being shuffled about. And then in a clear voice, volume increased in degree so that Gabriel was able to hear the entire conversation, words of apology came through the open areas of the splintered boards. "Oh, excuse me, Mrs. Mouse. I didn't mean to disturb you. I'll be out of your way in just a minute." At this announcement, Gabriel shook his head and had to seriously question his own mind about why he was still remaining at this site and more so, what kind of person this woman who was now talking to mice, really was. He was distracted from his self-examining thoughts as his attention ricocheted once again to the ensuing clamor that was coming from behind the weather-washed boards. A bump on the crippled portal caused it to wobble from the subsequent intrusion but the vulnerable appendage had obviously decided to hold its stand even as it was being tortured from inside. And then the final words of the soliloquy…"Ah, there you are. I knew you'd still be here."

As Gabriel stared at the corner of the garage, he watched in bewilderment as the woman came once again into his view. So laden was she with her arms full of "who knew what" and her hair and clothes covered with such copious amounts of dust, cobwebs, and unidentifiable debris that Gabriel hardly recognized the prim lady he had met only moments ago.

Walking to the center of the drive, the woman dropped the heap of whatever it was she was carrying, and proceeded to shake and brush off the coating of webs, string, feathers and all the other collectibles that had gravitated and adhered magnetically to her person as she scavenged through the piles of junk that inhabited the familiar old spaces.

"Now we can get serious about this task before us," she said after pulling what was hopefully the last remaining spider web from her cropped gray hair, a hairdo that Gabriel Phillips initially surmised did make the woman look quite sporty even if she didn't know anything about sports. But now, that hastily drawn summation seemed to be settling in for a challenge to prove him wrong!

"There's nothing like a good game of tennis to get the blood flowing, the heart pumping, and just generally give a healthy boost to the system. Plus… it gives old ladies like me a chance to, as you young folks say...strut my stuff." At the conclusion of this statement, Angela raised her heels and jounced in place with a several quick steps. Between bounces, she paused briefly to elicit a wink to the stunned, entranced figure posed rigidly before her.

The constricted smile that accompanied the wink gave Gabriel cause to shrink back a step. No, it was more like a giant leap backwards as he was jolted into the realization that he would indeed have to re-think his preconceived evaluation of this very unique individual who had just stepped into his life, or rather, bounced into it. She was energy personified. Was she for real? His better judgment told him she was indeed real and he had a feeling that he was about to learn *how* real.

—

The tattered bundle of netting, which was now draped across the pebbled drive, more closely resembled a sieve than a barrier for wayward hits, but it was soon displaying proof that it still had some worth left in its frayed strings and gaping holes. Only one time during all the answered returns did the ball find an escape route and even then Angela had scooped it up with finesse plus a few pebbles and returned it to her astonished young partner.

The scarred wooden tennis racket that had been retrieved from a nail in the old garage still had some life in it, as did its owner. While she had eventually over the years progressed to the modern graphite rackets, Angela found that this old standard of hers not only could still do the job, but in some ways it gave her an immense feeling of comfort and seemed capable of returning her to the exhilaration of her former days of competition. This young man had brought her more than just the joy of watching his performance. He had brought back her competitive nature. After all those years of helping others reach their goals, she now found the drive of that desire returning to *her* in a most exhilarating way. Well, what to do about that! Unknown yet even to her, a plan was being formed.

—

"Hey, kid." At the sound of voices and wheels skidding to a halt on the gravel road next to the deteriorated sidewalk, Gabriel took his eye off the game and looked to his right. As he did so, he felt a thump on his shoulder as the tennis ball met a target. His attention was immediately drawn back to the woman who had sent the volley his way. "Lesson number one," she said sternly, but patiently, while holding up the index finger on her left hand, "never let any outside disturbances influence your flow of play. Your competition can plant distractions anywhere and it could cost you the game." He saw the corners of her mouth rise suggesting a forthcoming smile and felt foolish that he had taken his train of thought from the court action. "Go ahead," she offered, while waving him toward the newly arrived audience, "see what your friends want. We've done enough for one morning."

"Oh, I'm sorry about that," Gabriel said as he retrieved the escaping ball, "I was just so surprised to hear... They're not my friends, though, at least not yet. I haven't met anyone since we moved here."

"Well, then maybe it's time you do. I'll just gather up all this old stuff here and be out of the way. But I...I will see you here again tomorrow morning, same time, won't I?" Angela held her breath in waiting anticipation, hoping he had enjoyed the early day routine as much as she had.

"You ...you want to do this again? I mean...you want...you and me...? Here?" For some reason Gabriel couldn't believe this stranger wanted to help him, was willing to spend some time helping him improve his game. From what he had gathered while the pair had hit back and forth over the frazzled net, was that this was no amateur he was pitted against. And for her to take such an interest in him didn't seem possible. Did he want her to show up again tomorrow morning? Did he want to play tennis every day of his life? Both questions went without asking.

"Yes," Angela went on, "I would very much like to continue where we left off today. Well, maybe not with you chasing that stray ball around, but rather have you right up by this net to see if you can put your full concentration on the game at hand." She smiled coyly as she finished speaking.

Noticing the sheepish look that had briefly lowered the young man's eyes to the ground, Angela waved her arm at him, shooing him toward the three youths who stood straddling their bicycles as they kicked away an occasional stone for no other reason than to be doing something. Their quizzical attention, as they waited acknowledgment of their presence, was divided equally between the newest teenager in town and the "old lady" who, rationalizing with their immature minds, should be sitting on a porch shucking peas or making rugs out of old hunks of material, instead of standing on an old patch of rocks batting at tennis balls. A totally absurd situation in their eyes.

As Angela gathered up the net and the two broom handles she had woven through each ribbon-bound end to hold the netting into the ground, she heard fragments of sentences coming from the small group gathered on the road. "…new here, aren't you? …why…old lady?…looks like someone's grandma…slippers…Want to …tennis at my place?…dad's the doctor in town…my own court…you don't have…old ladies!"

Angela glanced over at the boys and saw Gabriel looking back over his shoulder in her direction as he gave her a wave. He appeared to be a mite unsettled as he turned once more toward the visitors and she heard him say in a voice heavily laced with reprimand, "You know, guys, I'm new in this town, and I haven't met anyone my age yet, but if everyone around here is as rude as you three seem to be, maybe I won't be too anxious to meet anyone else. First of all you're intruding on my lessons, second you're making remarks about a lady who could probably whip all three of you at this game and third… After Gabriel's second statement, Angela heard a few "Yah, right. Sure. Whatever you say, new kid." And "What do we look like…a bunch of beginners?"

Well, enough of that. Angela took note that Gabriel had at that point decided the welcoming group had stepped over an intensely drawn, albeit invisible to the common eye, boundary line and she listened as he presented one last retort. "Forget it guys. I was hoping you were going to be friendly, and possibly show me around this town a little, but I think I might be better off checking it out myself. Maybe I'll see you another time when you have something good to say."

With that declaration hanging heavily in the humid morning air, Gabriel left the encounter, cradling his racquet underneath the pit of his left arm. Returning to the graveled drive he took the net and poles from Angela and carried them to the side of the garage.

Cautiously opening the invalid door, the young athlete stepped gingerly over the threshold onto the dirt floor. Setting the much used equipment back inside the building whose square footage, he quickly took note, was home to not only rusty lawn sprinklers, a single-wheeled garden plow, a solo nine-buckled rubber boot, but was also the much treasured abode for the grandly revered Mrs. Mouse.

The four-legged resident peeked cautiously over a discarded wheel rim as Gabriel settled the netted paraphernalia next to what was most certainly another vintage piece of equipment. His youthful eyes didn't hold any sign of recognition. At the end of a long wooden handle, the contraption had an open cylinder held in place by two medium-sized wheels. The inside of the horizontal piece was filled with a configuration of crooked blades. He wondered what modern invention had replaced this hand-propelled relic.

Angela watched the young man as he came back to stand on the drive next to her. There was a look on his face of someone determined to set matters straight, not just with her, but in his own mind as well. He spoke in a tone that inferred absolute resolution.

"I'm sorry if you heard any of that exchange, but I do not care one whit if they're doctors' sons, lawyers' nephews, or even the mayor's offspring, no one, and I mean *no* one, has the right to be inconsiderate and rude. And, further more, I don't care if they have the only tennis court in town. I'd rather play against this garage, or over that wounded net in there," he exclaimed as he pointed toward the object insinuated, "than play with a team of ingrates like that. Now… is six o'clock tomorrow morning still on?"

It was now the adult's turn to stammer and she did it with expertise. "Well…well, I…I…yes…um… yes of course, it's…it's still on. I'll…I'll see you right after sunrise." For once in her life the lady seemed not to be in control. This young man who had appeared intricately discombobulated when she had first approached him earlier, had suddenly metamorphosed into a natural born leader. She was impressed, and surprisingly, almost speechless.

The teenager picked up his jacket and flipped it over his shoulder all the while holding tightly to the tennis racket that had never left his person. It had remained attached to him, tucked snuggly under his left armpit as he had walked over to meet the local town youths and also as he had stashed away the fragmented netting. Angela watched as the boy ambled over to the time-affected pathway, exuding waves of confidence as he made his way toward the village's business section and, undoubtedly, to his family's new living quarters, wherever they might be. Her reaction to the sight was a shaking of her head as she found herself wondering where that sudden spurt of self-assurance had come from. He reminded her of someone else she knew. Someone she knew personally, very personally indeed.

—

With silence now surrounding her, Angela turned back to look at the area that had until a few short minutes ago been filled with the sounds that had been a such an integral part of her life these past many decades. She couldn't imagine living without them. Oh, she trusted that the boy would return tomorrow, of that she felt completely confident, but what about the next day, the next week? Not that he wasn't going to continue with his playing, but he would eventually come to terms with the young men who had stopped by this morning, or if not them, there would be others. And, of course, that's as it should be. But she just couldn't see herself not being a part of the action she had grown so accustomed to all these years. If only there were some way to keep…

And then, as if an egg commenced hatching right before her eyes, the answer presented itself as a predestined awakening. It was the logical next chapter in the journal of her life. The curtain that revealed the future was rising and as it did, Angela watched as the ancient vacated lot transformed itself into a stage of action, competition, hard work, power, energy. She felt a familiar tingle return to her body as she envisioned the anticipation on the faces of the challengers, the exuberance radiating from each excited participant, the cheers of the observing crowd. Once again the former instructor became rejuvenated with the spark that had ignited her own wick of energy during those times when she seemed surrounded by unfathomable shadows of memory.

Apparently looming deep within her mind the past several days, there had been a gathering of thoughts tumbling about searching for release. If she had allowed herself to disperse some of those very thoughts she had had while gazing out the living room window on her first full day back in Blooming Grove, she would have realized that already on that day ideas were taking root that would put vibrant life back into the sullen grounds that reclined lazily across the street from her yellow bungalow. As one looked at the place now it was difficult to visualize that in days long past it had been vibrantly alive with continual sounds of laughter, gaiety, activity. Special people sharing special times.

And now, because of one young stranger, who for some inexplicable reason didn't seem like a stranger at all, the former tennis instructor had found the solution to retrieving the joy of those exhilarating days. It had been so simple and yet if it hadn't been for Gabriel Phillips, and the arrogant, not to mention the uncouth delivery, of the informative words of the visiting trio, Angela Wellerman might never have thought of a solution to the puzzle. Sometimes the youth of the day unintentionally give the youth of yesterday that drop of fuel needed to relight a dying flame. Angela felt duly refueled and with one last look and nod, turned away from the deserted spot that would very soon be transformed from graying staidness to an area of colorful unleashed activity. She couldn't get to City Hall fast enough.

—

The morning workouts continued daily, even on Sunday mornings. A lot of hits could be gotten in before the pealing of the church bell. Nothing, though, could interfere with the peaceful moments of gathering together and giving thanks for all the blessings received during the week. And the blessings that had been heaped upon Angela Wellerman as of late deserved more than just an occasional response. She was thankful every day, repeatedly, for the bounty she was harvesting since her return to the place where nearly half a century ago she had experienced what now seemed like a distant dream. But it remained teetering on the far edges of her heartstrings, ready to topple into her memory at any given moment.

There had been that one tender, loving night. A lifetime ago. A starlit moment in time that usually only takes place on a movie screen or within the bindings of a dreamy romance novel. It was intended to have been only the beginning of a fulfilling life of happiness, eternal devotion, enduring love. But then in one tragic, nightmarish sequence of events on a desert landing strip, that melding promise of everlasting bliss was wiped out. A stirring loneliness crept into its place, keeping vigil in the darkened shadows of time. The haunting emptiness seemed to have no bounds.

But, now in the most unlikely of circumstances, that hollow part of her, that for all those years had held echoes of loss that vibrated intensely throughout her shaded existence, was now, in ways she couldn't explain, being challenged by an intrusion of youthful freshness and Angela found herself relishing in the healing changes that it was bringing to her scarred memories.

Angela didn't reveal to Gabriel her plans until after their first week of workouts and then one morning it naturally just fit into their conversation as the hour of practice ended. When tightening the net after their play, (they had decided not to take it down each day since it seemed to inherit a new open area every time they stretched it into place), Gabriel's fingers caught on one of the webs of frayed strings, and when he wriggled them free, the whole side of the net pulled away from the ribbon. His forthcoming apology was interrupted by laughter from the other side of the net.

"It looks as if this might be one of last days we'll spend playing over this net, Gabriel. While its true that this flimsy old web of string has a lot of sentimental attachments clinging to it, that's about all it's capable of holding these days. But even considering its years of abiding devotion, I think it's time to make other arrangements, don't you?" Angela looked questioningly at Gabriel, waiting for a reply.

"Well, I…I guess that might be a good idea," he said, although the tone of his voice betrayed the sincerity of his answer, "but you're right about the sentimental part. This one does hold some special memories, even for me now." A vision of the new net Angela must be intending to purchase stretched before Gabriel's eyes. "Then, again, if you…ah…if you think it's best, I guess I could adjust."

With that statement of surrender, Gabriel's face lit up with the smile that now was a most familiar sight to Angela. The glow of it spread a layer of warmth over a heart that over the years had become accustomed to the chill of lingering solitude. It was the way of life she had chosen, this was true, but the icy surface that had formed over her deeply wounded feelings so many years ago had shown no promise of melting. That is, there had been no sign of change until this sparkling ray of sunshine had come into her life a few short weeks ago. She now felt the arrival of a new season coming on, one that would lift the lingering fog, allowing her to enjoy once again the cloudless days and starlit nights.

"Well, perhaps now is as good a time as any to tell you about the plan in progress before you hear all the noises and disturbances that will be coming from here starting tomorrow." Angela held back a smile and waited for a reaction. She got one, but not the one she was expecting. Gabriel's face suddenly became paved over with a thick coating of unbelief and despair. As she heard the next words he spoke, Angela chastised herself for not just blurting out the plans for the future project instead of skirting around it to prolong the suspense and surprise.

"Oh, no, have...have you sold the lot? Is...is someone is going to build a house here? I mean, I know it's your property and all, but...well..." Devastation seemed to fill every pore on the boy's face. It was only a game, he knew that, but the hours he had spent learning and appreciating the talent of his mentor, well, he wasn't ready to have them end.

"Whoa there, young man. I'm not doing this very well. I'm sorry." Angela interrupted, holding up her hand to stop him from going on with his erroneous conclusion. "There I go again, thinking people can read me like a fluorescent highway sign. I even thought you might have guessed by now, but this well-seasoned brain of mine isn't always at its most astute for reasoning. Yes," she quickly went on in order to ease his abiding trepidation, "someone is going to build on it, but that someone is *me*. And it's not going to be a house, but rather something that you and I, and hopefully many others, will be able to enjoy for years to come. Gabriel, I'm having a tennis court built right here, right on this very spot where we're standing and tomorrow is groundbreaking day. Does that meet with your approval?"

If there had been a camera within her reach, Angela would have had available for her portfolio a progressive series of reaction shots to be envied by even the most highly specialized photographers, a presentation that heretofore had never been put on film. She could see the projected award winning sequence as it faded from a visage of lowly despair, moving sequentially to an image of gentle confusion, hesitantly bouncing as it jumped to pale enlightenment, cautious disbelief, and finally succumbing to the prize-winning finished portrait... exalting jubilation. And to enhance said display, the "piece de resistance," a moving panorama of a young man struggling to erase each singular emotion in order that he might replace it with a final image that would allow him to speak after having his senses so completely jostled.

Angela couldn't remember ever feeling so rewarded from anything she had ever done, not even in all her years of teaching. To have witnessed such a display of raw, unfettered emotions was overwhelming and she was momentarily taken aback as she felt a rare, stray tear escape to make its unbridled journey down

145

her cheek. Trying to be nonchalant in the spell of the moment, she brushed her hand quickly across the dampened trail, as if only in a casual swipe and then spoke as steadily as she could.

"Well, does that mean I have your approval for the project?" she asked, managing to emit a smile as the words came forth.

In a flash of movement, accompanied by an unintelligible whoop of delight, Angela felt herself constricted in a bear hug while being lifted several inches off the ground. It was hard to decipher who was more surprised over the uninhibited display of excitement, the silver-haired philanthropist or the exuberant muscled teenager, who when realizing what he had done, gently lowered the wide-eyed instructor to the ground and stood mesmerized, owl-eyed, speechless and filled with disbelief over what he had just done.

With his hand pressed tightly over his mouth, his face turning a deepened shade of fuchsia, Gabriel Phillips stammered a somewhat muffled makeshift apology. "Oh, Miss Angela…ah…that is, Miss Wellerman, I'm sorry. I don't know what got into me. It's…it's just that…well, I mean, it's… are you *really* going to put in a…a tennis court? I mean, wow, that's…that's terrific. That's…wow. I can't believe you're really…wow!"

"I…I take it that…that the 'three wows' mean you…you approve of the plans?" The excitement that Gabriel was eliciting seemed to transfer fluently to Angela as she heard a few double syllables of her own spilling forth as she spoke. "And I'd appreciate it if you didn't…didn't apologize for that display of exuberance. It isn't every day a lady my age is hugged by a handsome young man such as you, and I might add, it was most complimentary. A lot of the teenagers today think that people in my age category have been dropped stealthily to earth from some foreign planet and if they just ignore our presence we'll eventually return to our native homeland." Angela smiled once again, this time with more ease, and was rewarded instantly with a reciprocal reaction.

Gabriel recovered quickly from his ebullient physical outburst and spoke in a voice that remained filled with a high degree of astonishment. "I have to admit, I'm finding it a little hard to comprehend that there actually is someone on this earth, much less in this town, who is so kind, generous and talented and that I have had the good fortune to come in contact with her, ah, that is... with you. If I hadn't trespassed on your property..." With this inference, Gabriel saw Angela tilt her head down a fraction while giving him a look that implied they had already been down that route and it was an issue not be referred to again. Gabriel sheepishly mouthed an "I'm sorry"... not for the trespassing bit but for bringing up the matter at all. He was still dealing with the astounding turn of events than had evolved since that morning several weeks ago when he had happened upon this sparkling introduction to his life...one most inspiring, amazing lady whose friendship was becoming more treasured by him with each passing day.

—

When Gabriel had told his parents about the lady who had appeared mysteriously at his side that one sunny morning soon after their arrival in Blooming Grove to offer constructive criticism, freely and willingly, they reminded their only child to be polite and be sure to thank her for the advice she offered. And perhaps when they were settled in their new house, and when his father had returned from his extended business-training program, maybe she, Miss Wellerman, would consent to paying a visit to their home. They looked forward to meeting the person who was having such a positive influence on their son and to offer their gratitude for the advice she was giving him.

Well, as teenagers are wont to be, Gabriel just didn't know how to go about asking his mentor if she would like to stop over sometime and meet his parents, after all, maybe she would say no, and besides, his father would be gone for another week yet, so he had let the days drift fleetingly by while he enjoyed the instruction she offered, and the camaraderie they shared which seemed to hold a natural bond. He would ask her soon. He really wanted his parents to meet her so that they, too, could see what a special person she was. There was just something about her that he felt certain his mother and father would feel too. A binding link was forming, becoming stronger, as they spent more and more time together. How that could happen between two complete strangers, Gabriel couldn't understand. But for some inexplicable reason, they just didn't seem like strangers.

As the construction of the new court came to fruition, Gabriel and Angela stood on the graveled street visualizing the finished product. Their excitement was not contained, but rather it escalated in leaping degrees as they watched the daily progress. They exchanged enthusiastic remarks about the first match that would be held after the nets were set into place.

Since their old practice ground was now being dug up, making way for the new, the pair of competitors was relegated to hitting over the weathered picket fence that bordered Angela's backyard garden. Points were docked if either player hit the pointed tip of a fence post, or knocked off a ripening tomato. This set of rules forced them to be most diligent in the shots they volleyed over the 100 square feet of maturing vegetables. It admittedly wasn't the preferred mode of training for such an invigorating game, but the feat was challenging and what's more they found they were drawing an elusive audience.

Nearly every morning shortly after they started their garden routine, there would appear in their peripheral vision, movement near the sidewalk that bordered the yellow bungalow. Without glancing full on at the three curious sightseers, there was no doubt about their identification. The probing tentacles of curiosity were apparently at work. Buried within a mound of unsavory quirks was the haughty attitude displayed near a vacant lot those several weeks ago; taking its place was a driving desire to find out what all the commotion was about in an area of town where nothing ever changed except the height of the weeds.

An adhering magnet seemed to be attached to the trio, drawing them back daily now to check on the progression being made on the once orphaned lot. But it seemed even greater interest lay in catching covert glimpses of the strange event that took place early each morning across the street from all the noisy activity. The onlookers were not adept in disguising their unfettered interest. The sneering look of criticism toward a tennis-playing grandmother and her youthful partner seemed to have vanished as quickly as the dilapidated old garage had when pounced upon by that powerful razing piece of machinery. It was this peering inquisition that gave birth to the village event that would be responsible for changing forever the lives of its most recent arrivals.

—

Gabriel had grasped Angela's second plan with an enthusiasm that generated sparks to everyone he encountered as he spread word throughout the small town. He especially wanted to get the news out to the youths who had tried to show their daunting superiority at their first introduction. They still wore their nonchalant features whenever anything was mentioned about the new court, but at the same time continued what they believed to be latent surveillance of the town's latest construction project. Gabriel wondered if they would put their glowing praises of themselves to the test.

Before the court was even completed, Gabriel was posting announcements and sign-up sheets in each of the local places of business. The proprietors welcomed the upcoming event with an outpouring of support. For years the local chamber of commerce had been trying to get a public tennis court, not just for the youngsters of the community, but also for the "youthful" older villagers. Exercise was a staple for all ages. To their dismay, though, the endeavor had always fallen short of the votes needed to get the proposal under way. But now one of their own had returned and was generously taking on the project single-handedly. They meant to give full support to have this inaugural event be a success.

Signs went up. Everywhere! Mike's Barber Shop, Kelly's Pool Hall, Ernie's Grocery, Blooming Grove Creamery, Walt's Feed and Seed, Kay & Lynn's Thrifty Gifts, George's Hardware, Robbins' Bobbins (a sewing machine parts distributor). Even Herman's Funeral Parlor allowed a sign to be put up. There was only one request. Could the notice be on a plain white piece of paper instead of the standard neon pink? Request granted.

No other store window went without one of the shouting pink notices. The only thing missing was a list of participants to play in the one-day invitational doubles tournament. There needed to be four sets of doubles partners. With a single court, there wouldn't be room or time for more than that. Now Gabriel would finish his part of the project.

After asking the barber for directions, Gabriel walked to the outskirts of town until he came to a secluded lot surrounded on three sides by a forest of gigantic pines. Tucked back into the majestic setting was a two-story white brick house that was the residence of the local doctor and his family. Making his way up the lengthy cobbled path, the young man approached the mammoth double doors. Painted with a coat of bold vermilion, the twin entries brought the white exterior to full alert. Gabriel was reaching toward the brass doorbell when he heard, coming from the back of the house, the telltale sound of a bouncing ball. Leaving the stone walk, he went around to the side of the impressive work of architecture and immediately his vision came in line with that of three familiar forms.

He swallowed deeply, working up courage as he approached the fenced—in court. All eyes looked at him, silence and wariness in their wake. What ever had made him think he could do this? A natural instinct sent his reflexes into action and he started to turn away from the scene. But just then a picture flashed before him. A vision of a woman who represented determination, gentleness, strength, talent. Opportunity offered. Experience given freely. He turned back toward the challenge, finding the words he wanted to relay.

"Hi...Hi there." Waving his hand barely above his waistline, the uninvited visitor moved in closer to the wired play area. Swallowing once again to get rid of the lump in his throat, Gabriel inched ahead. "Ah...re... remember me? I'm the guy you approached a couple weeks ago about...about playing tennis. I was hitting around with Ang...Miss Wellerman...and anyway, we...or rather Miss Wellerman has put up a tennis court across from her house, maybe you've seen it..." (maybe indeed!) The three seemed to be transfixed at courtside, not acknowledging anything Gabriel was saying, but he kept right on talking anyway. After all, could anyone really be so rude as to not at least admit his presence? Well, maybe. But then he had started this thing and he had no intention of walking away without some kind of answer to his invitation.

"Perhaps you've seen the…the signs around town about a tournament, a…a doubles tournament to be held on Labor Day. Well, from what you said that day at the edge of the woods, it sounds as if you're all pretty good …ah…tennis players and we, that is, Miss Wellerman thought it might be a good way to initiate her court by having a small tournament. After the match she is going to officially donate the court to the village so it will be available for anyone who wants to play there."

No response from behind the fence except for an occasional shifting of balance as the trio appeared impatient about the interruption to their game. Gabriel ignored the slight and continued. "Well, the reason I'm here is that she…ah…that is…*we* were wondering if you three could find partners and join us in the tournament that day?"

As soon as the words were out of his mouth, echoes of laughter shattered the air. After the first burst of guffaws subsided, the doctor's son held his side as if hurting from the elicited efforts, but managed to speak between breaths. "You mean you want us to compete against you and that old… er, that lady?" The look on the youth's face was one of absurd incredibility. "Surely, you jest?" he said, apparently trying to show some form of literary savvy. When he saw that Gabriel was not backing away from the invitation, he went on. "Kid, there would be no contest. The three of us were all-conference champions this past year and I went to the state tournament in Bloomington. I think you're out of your league, "Gabby,"…or whatever your name is."

Ignoring the intentional jab, Gabriel went on. "My name is Gabriel," and I'm not saying we won't get beaten, it's just that, well…" And then a fuse dangled before his eyes and he found the spark to light it. "Well," he repeated, as he shrugged his shoulders, "I guess if you aren't up for the challenge I'll go over to Farmington and see if they have any players who'd like to sign up. I've heard they have some talented players over there. Sorry to have bothered you." With that concluding statement, Gabriel turned around to head back toward the walkway. Before he reached the cobblestone path, though, he heard heavy footsteps behind him and felt the vibrations of the ground as the three young men came to a jolting halt right next to him.

"Wait a minute there, Gab…er… Gabriel…I…I never said say we didn't want to play. We were just trying to figure out how we could hold back so you and the old…ah… the lady… wouldn't look too much like beginners. Unless, of course *you* have been holding out on *us* and you're both really trophy cup winners." Another round of laughter erupted. His two buddies slapped the doctor's son on the back as they congratulated him for his prized sense of humor.

"You're looking at your challengers, kid. We know three other players who will just love beating…sorry, I meant to say *playing,* you and your senile… ah…elderly lady partner. Put us down for the big event. We'll write our names down and get the list to you this afternoon yet so you can get the winners names spelled right on the trophy." Laughter vibrated the air one more time as the three young men became enthralled with what they considered comedic genius.

Gabriel left what was no doubt known as the prestigious end of town and walked toward the yellow bungalow to tell Angela that he had been successful in getting the parings for the tournament. The laughter that lingered on the trail behind him was suddenly reduced to a mere echo by the competitive thoughts that were pushing to the forefront of Gabriel's mind. Just wait, guys, just you wait. You *might* beat us, but then again...you might *not.*

The next morning the list of contest participants was posted on the storefront windows of each place of business throughout the town. Angela had printed a poster-sized notice that she tacked onto the telephone pole situated just off to the side of the newly constructed court.

———

The day of the tournament dawned with heavy humidity blanketing the early morning air. Angela awoke feeling exhilarated, yet aware of the gnawing tension that had always made its presence known in the preceding hours of all her personal competitions. Get a grip, Angela, she reproached herself. It's just a small town tournament. It's not a national competition. But once a competitor, always a competitor. She knew that was how it was and always would be. Not just for her, fact proven, but also for numerous other athletes who had been fierce challengers for a good portion of their lives and who could just never quite find release from that deeply seated trait.

Perhaps it wasn't so bad to keep some of that competitive drive, but it could make for some difficult challenges when the performer wasn't quite as agile in each precise move as he or she had been during the peak of a sparkling career. Expectations suffer then and it takes a lot of convincing to pull back and realize that everyone does have a set of new limitations. But, Angela concluded, *she* wasn't at that stage yet, not by a long shot!

Executing her spirited Rocky Balboa foot dance (was she slowing down a little on that? No, she assured herself mentally, and then repeated the word out loud for reassurance. "No!") Angela made her way to the entry door that would lead her out and over to a scene that had been a part of her life for over half a century. The former medal winner could still feel the bounce of her ribbon-tied ponytail against the back of her neck as she had when making her way from the locker room to the antiquated cement courts to vie for the high school conference championship. Deep inside she didn't feel any older than she had at that time.

Wasn't it interesting how you could look in the mirror and see a difference in your features year after year, but somehow if you could just reflect what you were inside, you would be surprised to see that hardly any changes had transpired at all. But it took years of living and experiencing to realize that.

—

As Angela crossed the graveled street she saw a crowd approaching from the center of town. A small group of people had also gathered around the handmade sign she had put up last night on the telephone pole. On closer scrutiny, she saw that it was the doctor's son and his friends. Apparently something on the sign was causing a bit of entertainment for the gathering. She could hear the laughter and caught several remarks of, "Well, that will be a hard doubles to defeat. Maybe we should all play under protest." Another outburst of laughter.

Angela's initial thought was that graffiti had been applied to the hand printed sign and was hoping it wasn't anything demeaning or censorial. As she walked over to the posting, the boys saw her. They made a quick exit, smirking in unison as they walked toward the newly constructed court.

Her first glance at the sign didn't reveal anything that looked out of place. No additional writing. No caricatures. The opponents were all still as she had listed them. Doubles #1: Allan and Mitchell. Doubles #2: Alexander (the doctor's son) and Leland. Doubles #3: Dean and Jaye. Doubles # 4: Angel Gabriel. Angel? What happened to the… Oh, so that's what had been the butt of entertainment. Angel Gabriel.

The moist early morning air had apparently taken liberty with one of the inked lines. The dew had washed off the trailing "a" from Angela's name while completely obliterating the "and" between her and Gabriel's names. Well, indeed, Angela had to agree, an opponent thus named would indeed be hard to beat, even with a two against one disadvantage, but the lady was determined that this twosome, talented Mr. Gabriel Phillips, and his partner (time to put the cards on the table) former national and world competitor, would be a difficult duo to conquer even without the revered title.

———

As the starting time of the tournament approached, the most experienced member of the competition became the recipient of a youthful jump-start. Glancing over at her partner, the former tutor was presented with a display of placid confidence that looked very familiar. It was most uncanny ...the striking similarity. Most uncanny.

Performing one more rendition of her "Rocky bounce," as she crisscrossed her tennis racket through the air, Angela allowed herself to drift into her competitive mode. Intentional detachment from the present surroundings kept her from seeing the congregated reaction to her light-footed dance. The opposing couples as well as the gathered audience responded immediately. There wasn't a closed mouth around the court. They gaped in unison at the reenactment, that is, everyone except Gabriel, who stood nodding his head at this mimicked display of rejuvenated energy. Here was tangible evidence to give credence to his suspicions.

Over the past weeks thoughts had been simmering on the back burner of Gabriel's mind. He couldn't seem to bring them to a full boil until now, when the brief preparatory dance had turned up the heating process. And then they had bubbled over in a profuse flow. There was most definitely a hidden talent in this person known as Angela Wellerman, waiting to pop its lid at the appropriate time. Apparently that time had arrived!

When the first match concluded, Angela began walking to her side of the court for the next contest.

Pausing briefly, she turned to scan the audience bordering the cemented layout. As her glance lightly skimmed over the enthused faces, she suddenly stopped, emitting a gasp. Who…? She darted her head back to the area that she had just passed over. But as she searched the spot frantically, the only thing that drew her attention was a woman leaning over the back of the bleachers handing a large thermos to someone on the ground. The space next to the woman was vacant. Chills prickled the skin on her arms and she momentarily stumbled as she stepped onto the court.

It wasn't the first time she had visualized his face in a crowd, but why now? She shook her head to clear it, but the feeling of uneasiness stayed with her. As she looked toward the opposite end of the net her glance met up with one from Gabriel. Seeing the worrisome look that had replaced his recent visage of confidence, Angela quickly assuaged it by waving off the incident with a reassuring smile and then leaned toward the ground to brush aside an imaginary stone.

—

After the match ended, Angela recognized an atmosphere of victory. The feeling of overall accomplishment, of well-earned success was in the surrounding air, but in all honesty she could not remember anything about the play. Her mind seemed intent to dwell on the face in the bleachers. Apparently she and Gabriel had won in three straight sets, because she didn't feel the least bit exhausted and Gabriel had a most satisfied, relaxed look on his face. Not so their opponents. The smug look was gone and they looked, well, shocked would be a good word, she guessed. The final match would start after a short break. Angela and Gabriel would be pitted against the doctor's son and his partner. It would be a good game, she was sure, but she needed to clear her head of all that had been passing through it during the last session of play.

—

Losing her usual power of self-control over her thought processes, the plaguing scene continued to play over and over again in her mind. So many years ago. So young. All the plans, all the dreams. True love for both of them the moment they had met. It had all happened so suddenly, and yet in their hearts they knew that it was real, that it was one of those times that are so special that you feared someone would come by to wake you and puncture the dream. Even fairy tales would pale when compared to the kind of love they had discovered. During one star spangled night, thousands of moons ago, an enchanted young couple had pledged their lives, their hearts, their bodies, their souls to one another. Had promised to live together, love together and through the magic of their love would show the world that even though they were earthly strangers only hours ago, they had somehow known each other since the beginning of time.

There had been no regrets. No guilt. No thought except that it had been natural, predestined. Their future was written on the stars. They reached for it and held it close. They embraced it because it was there. The future, the present, the past, they were all as one. They parted at daybreak that next day, that last day,

Angela having spent the night "with a friend," (her explanation to her parents) knowing the time would soon come when they would never have to be separated again. But that day was not to come. Not then. Not later. Not ever. Their first separation had lasted a lifetime. The fairy tale was missing a" happily ever after" ending.

Before leaving the small town that had given Jamie Austenson a love that he knew would last throughout eternity and beyond, before leaving for his assigned duty of service, the devoted young man had reached out to Angela, holding her tightly within his embracing arms. He couldn't find enough words to tell her how special she was to him. She was beyond special. She was a part of him, a part he couldn't live without. Angela knew his feelings without him even saying the words out loud because it was the same for her, but as he spoke she grasped each whispered syllable as if it were a newly discovered gem.

He couldn't seem to tell her often enough how much she meant to him. The adoration he held for her was so immense that he concluded that one heart would just not be enough to hold all the love he felt for her. And, as if once again there was proof that their future together had been plotted long ago, Jamie went on to tell Angela that at last he knew why he had miraculously been blessed with two separate hearts. It was because of her that he had been given the extra one; there was no doubt that the first one would be filled so completely with his feelings for her that he would need another one to collect the overflow that would accumulate over the many years ahead.

Angela had thought the declaration touching. Its intensity reached beyond the depths of her Cinderella dreams, even though she knew he was embellishing his numbers just to impress her. It didn't matter. The sincerity with which he had presented the twin lifelines was to her a gift of true devotion she would cherish all her days. He had found a way to put the crowning seal on their coming together. She felt more certain with each passing second that they had been brought together by a power neither could comprehend. It had happened and they embraced it.

Angela responded with a timid smile as Jamie looked at her, a puzzled frown crossing over his handsome young face. "What's the matter? Don't you believe I have two hearts?" She tried to conceal her unchallengeable doubt, but she knew she would never be able to keep anything from her Jamie. The twinkle in her eyes gave her away. Jamie went on. "Oh, so that's how it's going to be, is it? Do I see a hint of doubt in those cocoa brown eyes of yours? Well, young lady, step right over here and feast your eyes on this medical wonder."

A condescending look came over Jamie's face. Angela knew it was only a pretentious act and she wondered what he was going to do to prove his overblown braggadocio. He seemed determined to show this young lady that James William Austenson never tells a lie. Angela watched with intense curiosity, tongue in cheek, as Jamie reached his right hand over to his left shirtsleeve and began to roll it up. When he had it well above his elbow, he beckoned her with an index finger and with a Cheshire cat grin that widened with each step she took, he raised his eyebrows and said, "Okay, Miss Doubting Angel, what do you think now? Is this proof enough for you?"

Angela's glance lowered to his now partially bared arm. A few inches below the turned up sleeve was a reddish-brown mark that... Angela's eyes widened at the sight before her. There was indeed something there and it was in the shape of a valentine heart. No imagination was needed to see the resemblance. As she returned her gaze to Jamie, she no longer saw a smile, but rather a look that said, "I told you so."

Feeling bested, she shrugged her shoulders and sought an explanation. "Okay, Jamie, you win. I see it. Now tell me how it got there. Who...ah...when did you have it put...?

A chuckle escaped from deep within Jamie as he reached out to give Angela a hug, interrupting the questioning session. Releasing her, yet holding her near, Jamie told her no one had put it on there. He had always had it. He actually did have an extra heart. Angela listened in stunned silence as Jamie continued his explanation.

His father had one, his father's father had one and who knew how far back the pronounced birthmark went. "It's been a staple in the Austenson family for generations and I would wager that one day," he paused here to wink at Angela, and then continued as a sheepish smile added color to his animated features, "my...rather *our*... son will carry with him the exact same trademark."

All Angela could say after hearing his last statement was "Oh, Jamie." Her face began to blush, its pinkish hue matching that of Jamie's, as his words sent a reminder of the evening they had spent together.

She now dared to dream forward to the time when they would be able to live freely with the deep affection they felt for each other, a time when they could present to each other and their families the result of their love. Their own son.

—

How wonderful it would be if we could just write down a life plan and follow it step by step. It would be so easy, so satisfying. But there isn't a set program. There are last minute, last second changes. And often those changes disrupt the entirety of the original groundwork. And this was to be the outcome for the charted future of one young James William Austenson and his chosen mate, Angela Francine Wellerman.

Just when it seemed that a dream would soon evolve into reality, a nightmare moved in and erased that vision, destroyed that dream, leaving Angela to mourn young love and a new life that developed because of it.

The first of the promised daily letters had arrived one week to the day Angela and Jamie had met. Angela had been at the door when the mailman had delivered it so she had quickly taken it and gone to her room, hardly containing herself to keep from tearing it open before she was alone. The time would come soon enough when she would tell her parents about her plans. Jamie's and hers. She knew they would think she was too young, just having graduated from high school and now getting ready to go off to college on a tennis scholarship. They were so proud of her accomplishments and pleased that she had been rewarded for all her athletic talent and dedication.

The postmark showed the mailing date as one day after Jamie had arrived at the Air Force training base in Arizona. He was excited about the career he was embarking. A fighter pilot had been the only thing he had ever wanted to be since that magical Christmas morning when he had received his first toy silver airplane. He had been three years old.

As much as he had dreamed day after day, year after year of this plan, he now wasn't so certain it was a good choice. He went on to mention in the letter that maybe he would have to change his thinking if he was going to have a wife in the very near future. He didn't want Angela to have to worry about him every time he left to report for an assignment. Perhaps he would look for something that involved ground duty. Angela knew she would never ask him to forsake his childhood dream and found herself shaking her head to telegraphically reassure him and herself as she continued to read the letter.

Each line was filled in depth with details of the excitement Jamie was now experiencing. The early morning wake-up call, the exercise routines, the young men who were beside him as they received instruction on the routines that would now become an integral part of their lives on a military base. Angela stopped reading for a minute to reaffirm that never, never would she allow Jamie to bring up the subject again of not pursuing his dream. He wanted it and she wanted it for him.

The next lines that Angela read seemed to waver a bit. As she read them she could envision Jamie as he scrawled them onto the paper. His excitement showed through as the words slanted haphazardly before her eyes. He no doubt had written at a quickened pace, filled with enthusiasm for the news he was telling her. He couldn't contain his feelings. "Just imagine", he had written, "tomorrow will be a day I'll never forget. My first trip up in a fighter plane. My name was picked out of a list of new recruits to accompany two experienced flight instructors." "Of course," he went on to explain, he wouldn't be at the controls yet ("but wouldn't I love to be!") "Nevertheless, it will be the flight of a lifetime. I'll write tomorrow and tell you all about it. And just so you know," he continued, "I'll be thinking of you, my beautiful Angela, every second I'm up there. I'm sure "both my hearts" will be beating at the highest rate possible, each filled with loving thoughts of you."

Over the years the memory of holding and reading that letter had remained imbedded in her mind. It was the first one, the first of many she knew she would receive over the next months. When she had finished reading it that morning, she had folded it carefully, returning it to the pale blue envelope that proudly displayed an Air Force emblem in the top left corner. Walking over to the antique oak dresser, she had lifted the cover of the miniature cedar chest that sat atop it encasing her few pieces of jewelry. She placed the treasured leaflets at the top of the opened case, covering her silver charm bracelet and the single strand of pearls she had worn the night of her high school graduation only weeks ago. She knew she would be lifting that cover several times during the day to read again and again the letter's cherished contents.

She made a mental note that she would have to look for a larger container, perhaps a shoe box or several of them, she thought, as she smiled in anticipation of all the letters that would be coming to her from that far away base in Arizona. She even dared to think ahead to the day when he wouldn't have to write to her, because she would be right there with him. The future held so many bright, exciting promises and she couldn't wait to start gathering them all together. But she told herself not to think so far ahead, but rather to take the time to enjoy the present. Step by small step, stopping to appreciate the wonder of each.

But there had been no letter the next day, or the next. Angela was disappointed but knew that these were busy days and weeks for Jamie. He would write as soon as he was able to get some free time.

—

Angela usually read the Metro Tribune each day, but the last two days she had been thinking so much about Jamie and how he was doing, that she hadn't even skimmed the main headlines. But that third day after not receiving a letter, she had reached for the front page as she walked into the kitchen to fix a sandwich for lunch. It was a Saturday and her parents had left earlier that morning to go to an estate auction in a neighboring town. She had placed the newspaper on the round maple table, glancing briefly at several of the bold headlines. One that caught her eye was situated at the top of a column in the upper left hand corner of the daily paper. Its dark print displayed words that seemed to be getting more common each day. Inquiries. Investigations. It seemed there was never an easy solution to any of the tragic, and often mysterious, incidents that were taking place these days. Angela wondered what it was now that was being looked into. She always felt such a wave of sympathy for the people who had suffered or would be suffering because of this latest turn of events. Little did she know that it was a story that would affect the rest of her living days. She began to read:

INVESTIGATION UNDERWAY
AUTHORITIES ARRIVE AT ARIZONA AIR
FORCE BASE

Twenty-four hours after the crash of what was believed to be the most elite training bomber in the United States military, authorities from Washington D.C. arrived at a world renowned Air Force base near Phoenix, Arizona. The crash which occurred on the base Monday morning, killed two top flight instructors and one young trainee who had been selected from a list of new recruits to fly on a short trip to Albuquerque, New Mexico, and back. The young man's name is being withheld pending notification of his nearest...

That was all the farther Angela got on the article before she felt herself being enfolded in a gray cloud. She grabbed on to the edge of the table and lowered herself to the chair that sat near the table. It was all over. Somehow she just knew the dream had ended. She wouldn't need to see the name printed in the paper. She knew who it was. Oh, Jamie. Jamie. She felt a wave of nausea coming over her and ran quickly to her room. She was there only a minute when her abdomen retched with a trembling force. She made her stumbling way to the bathroom, getting down on her knees as she leaned over the porcelain fixture to release the pressure from deep inside the walls of her stomach.

The next two days Angela had stayed in her room, shades drawn to keep out the brightness of what would normally have been a cheery summer day. Her nearly 36 hours of occasional vomiting and accompanying weakness had convinced her parents that she had acquired an acute case of the summer flu. She had not told them about the article or what it had to do with her life.

On the third day after the initial onset, Angela had gingerly made her way downstairs to sit at the breakfast table with her parents before they left for work. Her mother worked as a volunteer at the local nursing home and her father had a small, but prosperous real estate office on the main street of town. They were both counting the days now when they could retire and do some traveling. Angela would be attending Northwestern College in the fall and it was important to them to be free to visit her and watch as she competed at a new level in her tennis competition.

Having her parents at courtside during her matches over the years had made Angela feel extremely fortunate. Knowing they were proud of her achievements by supporting her activities, gave her inspiration to reach higher goals each time she performed. Her mother and father had never pushed her to become the best in what she did, only to do her best in anything she tried. As her talent grew so did her self-discipline. Even though her coaches said she was a natural athlete, she never rested on her inherent talent. Practice routines were never shortened. When she felt she had reached a goal, she extended her expectations. Confidence exuded from her as she competed. Tension had no place on the court. The butterflies that fluttered briefly within her as match time approached were soon sent on their way as she walked toward the net. Landing in their place was the soaring exhilaration she felt as she saw her opponent's racquet take position for the first volley of the day.

—

Angela's mother and father knew that their daughter would of course need her space to adjust to campus life. They wanted her to enjoy her years as a college student, but it was a good feeling to know that if and when she needed them they would be available to make the trip at a moment's notice since they no longer would be obligated to the working world. The rewards for starting their family later in life held promises of even more rewards than they had already received. Little did they or she know that the changes about to take place would not be happening as planned. The days and months that lay ahead held challenges that would remold their lives forever.

Angela was an only child and she had been a complete surprise. The couple had accepted the fact that they would be childless after so many years without an answer to their prayers. And then one day Angela's mother, at forty-five years of age, was told at her annual physical that she should give prompt consideration to setting up a nursery in her home because in six months she was going to be adding a tiny new member to their quiet household. Angela was the angel of their lives.

—

Finally after spending several days confined to her room, Angela made an effort to join her parents at the breakfast table. As her father sat reading the daily sports page, Angela's mother brought a cup of steaming coffee over to the table and set it down next to her husband, rustling the morning edition as she did so. This had been her daily gesture for years, born out of necessity after having had a coffee soaked front page handed to her morning after morning. The only time she didn't have to get her husband's attention was when the Vikings had found a way to blow a 35 to 10 lead in the final 15 minutes of Sunday's game. The Monday morning sports page stayed folded just the way the paperboy had delivered it!

Angela took her usual place next to her father. As soon as the wafting vapors hit her senses, Angela felt the recognizable queasiness overcome her yet again. Pushing her chair quickly aside, Angela raced to her bathroom to relieve the building pressure. Perhaps she really did have the flu, not just the shocking results of loss and emptiness that had been thrust into her young life.

That afternoon, after spending several hours with a cold cloth on her forehead, and taking occasional sips of the ginger ale her mother had set on her bedside table as she had dozed, Angela forced herself to get out of bed. Throwing her robe casually around her shoulders, she made her way down the steps, going directly to the front door to check for the daily mail. While sorting through the several envelopes addressed to Mr. Arthur Wellerman and the occasional "Present Occupant" ones, her hand suddenly froze as she came across one addressed to Miss Angela Wellerman. The envelope had an Air Force emblem in the left corner. Relief filled every pore in her body as she tried to get her legs to move her back into the house. "Oh, dear God, thank you, thank you" she repeated several times as she held the letter close to her wildly pounding heart. "How foolish of me. I should have known he was just busy studying and adjusting. Sometimes there just isn't time to write."

She checked the return address one more time before turning the envelope over to open it. Her hand started shaking as a sudden chill passed throughout her body. It wasn't Jamie's name. It wasn't his writing. Why hadn't she noticed that? She had read his first (his only) letter so many times she had each individual dot, loop and swirl memorized. The name in the return address corner was Jason Anderson. Angela no doubt had just focused on the first initial of each name and hadn't looked beyond the two single letters. At the sight of the military emblem a tide of relief had washed over her and she had only thought about the loving words she would soon be reading.

Turning now to go back into the house, she stepped over the threshold but remained in the entry hall. She couldn't find the strength to push her feet forward to go any further into the room. Turning the envelope over, she shakily lifted the glued edge. As she pulled out its contents a snapshot floated to the floor near her feet.

Leaning down to pick up the black and white photo, Angela's heart jolted at the sight of Jamie standing next to the biggest airplane she had ever seen in her life. He was standing there with his left arm placed at an angle in front of him, his hand pointed at his heart. His right hand was directing her vision to the heart-shaped mark that was presented to him at his birth. His smile was so infectious she found herself smiling back at him.

As she peered more intently at the picture she noticed that his left eye was closed; he was winking at her. Just as he had done the morning he left Blooming Grove. Automatically, without intended thought, Angela turned the picture around. One just always expects something to be written there and, as anticipated, words covered the white background. The familiar handwriting burned into her eyes. "To my beautiful Angel(a). Angela smiled at that play on her name. "I will fly not only in the sky, but because of you I will fly on the earth, unable to get my feet to touch the ground. I love you with both of my hearts. Yours for all time. Jamie." The smile that had briefly touched her lips was gone. Just as her Jamie was gone. She felt emptied of life. This wasn't a love letter. It wasn't from Jamie.

Returning the picture to the envelope, Angela opened the sheet of parchment stationery. It was from Jamie's friend, Jason. The two young men had gotten to know each other over the past few years as they competed against each other during their high school baseball seasons. During their four years of eligibility their archrival teams, the Faribault Falcons and the Owatonna Indians had been the final two schools of the Big Nine conference vying for a berth to advance to the regional tournament.

While they had spent their high school careers on different teams, they were astonished to find out after their final game of competition against each other, that they were now going to be on the same team. Not for sports but for their country.

After shaking hands at the conclusion of the season, they had talked about the game and then casually started talking about their plans for the future. Not only had they been duplicates in their athletic talents, but they couldn't believe they had both enlisted in the Air Force and what was even more astonishing, would both be at the same training center.

They had gotten together several times during the following weeks to discuss their mutual interest for aviation, striking up a friendship that they anticipated would grow stronger as the months progressed.

During their last week of being civilians, the two young men decided to take a short trip around southern Minnesota. Maybe do a little fishing, say good-bye to some friends, check out some of the small towns they had never taken the time to visit during their busy high school years.

Their parents would meet them at the airport the morning of their departure, pick up the car they had used for their trip, and bring the extra suitcases they had packed before setting out on their farewell excursion.

—

Blooming Grove was a suburb of the Twin Cities, located about 30 miles south of the state capitol. As the two future pilots had driven along Highway 3 they came upon a blue rectangular sign on the right side of the road notifying them that they were entering the city limits of Blooming Grove. Driving up to the stoplight at the first intersection of town, another colorful sign caught their attention. It was a giant-sized invitation to "Visit the Dakota County Fair. One Week Only. Grandstand shows nightly. Demolition derby Monday, Wednesday, Friday and Saturday nights. The Biggest Midway This Side of The Rockies.

As Jamie had told Angela, it was just too tempting an invitation to turn down. A carnival might just be the way to top off their trip before heading for Wold Chamberlain airport early the next morning to board their flight to the military base in Arizona.

And that was when her life had changed, standing in line waiting to ride the Ferris wheel. It was Angela's favorite ride, but her friend, Susan, didn't like anything that went more than a foot off the ground so if she wanted to ride, she would have to go alone.

When it was her turn at the ticket window, she ordered one ticket, but as she was putting her change on the counter, a hand came around from behind her and several more coins were placed next to hers. "Make that two, please," a young male voice intruded. As Angela turned around she saw the most handsome boy she had ever seen. He smiled at her after leading her over to the empty seat that was coming down in front of them and said. "I noticed you were alone and my friend hates these things, so I thought maybe you wouldn't mind sharing a basket with me. I don't like heights much, but you look like someone who enjoys this ride so maybe you can console me if I get a little woozy as we spin around." Not until later in the evening did Angela recall Jamie's words. It was right after he told her he was leaving the next day for flight school! What a line...but she had fallen for it, hook, line, and sinker. Just as she had fallen for him.

Jason had wandered off to places unknown when she and Jamie had walked away from the midway that night. Friends intuitively knew when there were times they couldn't or shouldn't stick together. Angela never did find out where he had gone, but she did hear the next day that some young "out-of-towner" had cleaned out the entire stock of stuffed teddy bears from the softball-toss game booth. Jason?

—

All these distant memories plus more had occupied Angela's mind so that she hadn't even realized there was a tennis game in progress and that she was one of the competitors. She and her youthful partner hadn't won with her eyes closed, but they had won with her mind shutting out all but the thoughts of her past. Had she actually lived the past five decades during that one game? The "flu symptoms" that had lasted for nine months. Moving to Chicago. The home for unwed mothers that was managed by a close childhood friend of her mother's. Convincing her parents that she should not keep the baby nor could she accept their offer to take care of the child while she went on to further her education. They were near retirement. It would have been a difficult time for them raise a child under those circumstances.

No, she just couldn't let them do it. It had taken her many hours of anguish pondering but she had finally reached a conclusion that she thought best for all concerned. She wanted her baby, Jamie's baby, to grow up in a home with a father and mother who would be only a few years older than his or her natural parents. Oh, she knew in her parents' home there would have been an abundance of love and caring. Her parents had raised her under those cherished conditions and she had felt their love surrounding her every minute of her days. She had spent many heart-wrenching hours trying to convince herself that she could raise the child by herself, knowing that her parents would be near her to offer their unrelenting support. She never doubted the degree of love she would shower upon this new life, but the child deserved more.

There would always be questions. Where is the child's father? Were you married long? Do you feel capable of being both a father and a mother to your child? She couldn't do that to Jamie's child, her child. A complete family would give their son or daughter a better place in the world. At least at eighteen years of age she had thought so.

How many times over the past years had she wondered if the choice she had made was the right one? How many times had she regretted not allowing her parents the joy of playing with their grandchild? But she had made the decision and she prayed every night of her life that all had turned out well. If only she knew for certain…

Her parents had never seen the baby boy. She thought it better if they didn't. She knew she would never have been able to separate them once they had been together. But she had asked to spend a brief time with him alone before giving him to the adoption agency. She wanted, needed to see the beautiful life she and Jamie had created. To feel his soft skin. Count each finger, each toe. And to see for herself the one telling sign that would link the child to his father forever. To see if he had inherited the symbol of a lifeline.

And he had. It was there. The tiny reddish spot was clearly visible on the small, fragile arm of Jamie's son. Her heart skipped a beat as she rubbed gently over the mark. Her gaze became blurry, as tears spilled over cheeks. The warm, salty drops landed on the rosy hued area, symbolizing the baptism of the next generation. The new mother placed a gentle kiss on her son's forehead. As she brushed her hand lightly over the downy patch of dark hair that covered the tiny head she whispered Jamie's name. With a gentleness that seemed to be done in slow motion, she lifted the arm that displayed the small heart and placed it over his hidden one. "God take care of you, always, Austen William James. May you always feel the love that brought you into this world." A mother's tears once again baptized the gift of a new life.

Angela didn't remember the nurse coming in to remove the child from her arms, but she did know that if she had had a thousand hearts, they would all be breaking at this most hollow moment of her young life.

178

"An...Angela? Are...are you all right? Is something wrong?" The concerned voice of a young man brought Angela out of her reverie. As she looked up she saw Gabriel standing close to her with his hand timidly reaching toward her.

"What? What did you say?" Angela felt perspiration gathering at the back of her neck, but she knew she wasn't that warm. There was a cool September breeze blowing and she had a feeling the competition hadn't been great enough for her to overly exert. She lifted her hand to rub across the dampened area but her hand had come back dry. She was only warm under her skin. A vision of what had caused the emotional rise in temperature flashed before her eyes.

"Oh, Gabriel, I'm...I'm sorry. No, I'm just fine. I...I was just concentrating on the final match. Do you think our opponents are up to it?" She tried to sound as casual as possible while trying to slow down her pulse rate. What had set off that backtracking into her memory vault? She remembered looking into the crowd right before beginning play, but then couldn't recall anything that had taken place on the court after that. Was there someone there she had recognized? Hardly. Except for old Mr. Kelly in the pool hall, everyone else in town was new to her. Well, there was one more match to win. Time to step up to the net and show these youngsters that age isn't important when skill is involved.

And she was right. The harmonious duo polished off the match in record time. They graciously accepted the reluctant, but sincere congratulations of their opponents. When Alexander, the doctor's son, had finished shaking hands with Gabriel, Angela noticed that he leaned over close to Gabriel and in what was intended only for Gabriel's ears, heard him say in a sheepish, but genuinely sincere voice, "Does she have a friend her age who might be looking for a doubles partner? I…well, I could use a new one."

Gabriel let out a small chuckle and looking back at Angela gave her the most surprising response. He winked at her.

Oh, dear God. Dear, dear God. Was it possible? Is this why he seemed so…? She put her hand over her heart as she turned around. The crowd. The face in the crowd. She was afraid to look. She was afraid not to look. Could it be…? Angela's eyes focused once more to where she had glanced earlier, but there was no one there. As she searched over the other faces moving around the court, she suddenly felt a hand on her arm and heard Gabriel's voice.

"Angela, I have someone I would like you to meet. Dad, here she is. The lady I've been telling you about. Isn't she a terrific player? My dad's a great player, too, Angela; maybe you two should get together for a match sometime. What about it, Dad, wouldn't you like that and you too, Angela?" I think it would be the greatest…" Gabriel's voice became more animated with each word he spoke and the sentences started running together until finally his father interrupted.

"Slow down, Gabriel. I'd like to know if this talented lady has a voice as well as a great backhand. So you're the Angela my son has been talking about every night at the supper table. I'm pleased to finally meet you. My name is of course, "Dad," but I do have

180

another one. I'm Austen Phillips. And you are every bit the expert player Gabriel has said you are. I think I would like to sign up for some lessons from you when you aren't teaching my son how to beat his dad."

If Austen Phillips felt the trembling in Angela Wellerman's hand as he extended his to clasp hers, he no doubt chalked it up to the exhibition of enthusiastic play that his son and partner had just exhibited. The man was totally unaware that she had not heard another word he said after introducing himself.

Angela looked in stunned silence first at Gabriel and then at his father. She didn't really need the proof, but… Just then Gabriel let out a sudden gasp. His father turned toward him and noticed that his son was pulling up the left sleeve on his white Nike shirt.

"What's wrong son, is your arm sore? Should I get an ice pack?" The parental concern transferred to Angela. She inched closer to see if there was a problem that needed immediate attention.

"No, Dad, I think a mosquito just had its afternoon snack from my arm." Angela followed the movement of Gabriel's right hand as he rubbed it over the attacked surface. When he lifted his hand she saw the red welt but then…what was… there was something else. Another reddened area right above the raised spot. Had he been bitten twice? Or was this…could it be…? Angela's heartbeat seemed to have ceased its rhythm.

Seeing what appeared to Gabriel as a frown of deep concern on the face of his doubles partner, which seemed totally out of place for the minor attack that had just occurred on his arm, Gabriel quickly responded.

"He only got me once, Angela. Don't look so worried. It's just a mosquito bite. Are you looking at this other mark?" He didn't wait for an answer, which was just as well because there wasn't going to be one. Angela's thoughts were transfixed on the site before her. "Well, don't worry about that one. That's not a second bite. It's nothing. Well, not really nothing. It's just that it has been with me since day one. The stork delivered it the same day he delivered me. My dad has the same thing on his arm. Show her, Dad," Gabriel coaxed his father. With an edge of pride he added, "It's a true blue way to prove we're blood relatives. Isn't it great? C'mon Dad, show her."

"Gabriel, I hardly think, Miss...ah, Angela..." Austen Phillips began.

"Oh, but I...I would like to see it, Mr. Phillips. It sounds very in...intriguing. Like father, like...like son." She couldn't be breathing. She knew she couldn't be. But her heart was racing and pounding, so she had to be.

And then as the starched white sleeve was folded back...Angela saw her son for the second time in her life.

—

For the next few seconds the world was put on hold. Everything was moving in slow motion. She knew someone was talking but she had no idea who was saying it or what was being said. As the voices at last came out of the foggy distance and her vision stopped its waving motion, Angela felt her hand slip gently from the area over her heart as it moved in automation to her side.

Reaching into the pocket of her tennis skirt, Angela Wellerman removed the yellowed snapshot that she had carried with her every day since it had been delivered to her doorstep. She turned the photograph toward the two people who now stood before her so that the inherited smiles and the trio of identical lifelines might at long last be joined together. With a voice that was steady even as it filled with overwhelming love and joy, Angela Wellerman made the introduction that fulfilled her lifelong dream. The most treasured game of her life had just been won…when she was dealt the Three of Hearts.

JUST A SHORT NOTE...

July 10

Dear Cousin Loretta,

Just a short note to tell you how much we missed you yesterday at the annual Flomdahl family reunion. The Sogn Valley farmhouse had a hollow feeling wafting throughout its spacious rooms. The walls seemed to be bouncing off echoes of "Wherth's Lowetta? Wherth's Lowetta?" Oh wait, maybe that was Uncle Ole. If I remember correctly he didn't have his teeth in at the dinner. Anyway, I can understand how distressed you must be feeling after losing your precious Fluff Fluff. Every last one of us Flomdahls put our forks on hold for a moment of respective silence for that dearly departed feline. I do have one gnawing question that persists to jiggle around in my mind, though, 'Retta. How many lives does that darn cat have, anyway? I do believe (and I am keeping track in case you are thinking you can fool ALL your kin) that this is the eighth year in a row that Fluff Fluff has met his Waterloo! And it just seems to happen at the same time every year...right around reunion Sunday. I did bow my head at noon with all the other generations of Flomdahls in honor of that four-legged wonder's demise, but I'm on to you, Cousin. I kept silent this year, but you probably shouldn't count on my support once that cat uses up its nine lives. You owe me big time, Cuz.

Since circumstances completely in your control prevented you from suffering through the rituals with the rest of us, I'm taking great pleasure in telling you what you missed. I do hesitate slightly, however, in doing so, for fear ol' Fluff Fluff will borrow a few extra years from the neighborhood strays and find you with added excuses after next year, but I'll give it a whirl anyway.

Uncle Ole came duly armed with his obnoxious whoopee cushion, and once again put it under Aunt Tillie's chair pad. For a minute I thought Auntie had gotten a hearing aid because when she sat down on the cushion this year her face turned as red as Gramp's old Farmall, embarrassed, I surmised at the time, from the sudden, unexpected emission of gaseous activity that was generated when she took her designated spot at the table. Auntie proceeded to wave her hands about exuberantly, fanning the air that surrounded her side of the dining room table. I saw Uncle Clyde move his chair slightly to the left while giving his sister a disgusted look. His sibling returned the appraisal with a blank stare while sniffing the air inquisitively. God bless her. While Auntie's expression was one of lingering confusion, she intuitively shrugged her shoulders apologetically, although didn't appear certain that it was justified. She never looked up from her plate again during the rest of the meal so, of course, missed all the side glances that were directed her way each time a new rush of putrid odor hit the airwaves enveloping the dining guests.

I felt so sorry for Auntie, and would like to have gone upstairs to the bathroom to see if by any chance there was a bottle of Pepto-Bismol in that old metal medicine cabinet above the sink, hoping that a couple spoonfuls of that old reliable pink liquid would help ease her distress. (Have you ever looked in that cabinet? The last time I looked I found bottles of pills from the '30's and '40's in there.) But back to the point of excusing myself to check the medicinal contents of above mentioned cabinet. Well, as is the standard at every reunion dinner, chairs were jammed so tightly around the table that there was no chance of me getting up without taking a whole chain of Flomdahls with me. So I stayed in my assigned seat, willing that time would pass faster than the effervescent, exuding gas. The only one able to move around freely in that flowery-wallpapered room was Gramp's aged dog, Ralph, who seemed to have marked his spot right next to Aunt Tillie's chair.

Do you know that the wallpaper on those walls is still the same covering that was on there when we were little girls? Remember those days? When you came to every big gathering? Anyway, you can still see the stain left by the buttered roll that Uncle Halvor threw to Uncle Oliver during that one Christmas Eve supper.

When Uncle Oliver asked for the rolls, Uncle Halvor picked up one of the cloverleaf treats and after rubbing it between both his hands, reared back in perfect Cy young form and let loose with a soaring fastball pitch. Instead of landing in Uncle Oliver's open mitt, it flew over his head, sticking to one of the paper bouquets of roses sprawled over the wall. Gram scolded both of them profusely but when she was scraping the buttery substance off the wall I saw her upper body quiver ever so slightly and I have a feeling she was trying desperately to keep from laughing out loud so as not to give us youngsters any ideas about repeating the incident.

Those two uncles were always into some kind of shenanigans. But I do remember them coming up behind Gram afterwards to give her a big hug. She would try to look stern, but she wasn't a very good actress. Her twinkling eyes always gave her away.

I notice at every reunion, just before she sits down, she goes over to that greasy area and wistfully rubs her hand across it. I think the gesture temporarily transports her back to those lively days. We all miss those two jolly fun makers. God rest their souls.

Well, now, back to this year's gathering. As the mealtime progressed, I couldn't help but notice that the presenting foul air seemed to follow Gramp's dear, senile cattle dog around the table as he made his way from one Flomdahl to another. I watched as each Flomdahl relative in turn wrinkled up his or her nose as the old Collie strolled by, sticking his nose (I'm referring to Ralph here) under the hand-crocheted tablecloth waiting for the proverbial handout, that without fail at every reunion is the unidentifiable concoction that Aunt Clarissa brings for the potluck. The jury deliberating on this year's contribution is still out. And unless Ralph learns how to relay the final verdict it will remain an eternal mystery. The air surrounding that four-legged hand grenade yesterday held a jumble of clues but none that any of those attending the bountiful feast could decipher.

Poor Aunt Tillie. If she only knew that Ralph and Aunt Clarissa were the culprits responsible for giving her the soured reputation. And I feel a touch of sympathy for old Ralph, too. He must've suffered some horrific cramps, yet was able to come through seemingly intact in spite of all the ammunition that was passing through that aging intestinal tract of his. Ralph, Ralph, poor Ralph.

The rest of the meal was pretty much the usual spread. Aunt Josie brought her famous red Jello, with the "woody" fruit cocktail. Those hard chunks of pears once again had to be shifted past the molars about a dozen times before even a sliver could break loose. I've learned a trick over the years, though. While crunching the fruit-filled concoction, I casually pick up the napkin from my lap to wipe any traces of Jello that may have drizzled down my chin (her Jello never sets completely) and proceed to spit the miniature white logs into the cloth folds as the fabric crosses my lips. I then wait for Ralph to get to my side of the table. Good boy, Ralph.

Oh, yes, and what reunion could get away without a giant-sized pan of Aunt Serena's "prize-winning" (her claim only...I can't believe there's even the slightest hint of a blue ribbon anywhere in that disarrayed kitchen of hers) brownies. It's been rumored, by all who have dared to sample her bars, that there is the strong possibility that her pantry and medicine cabinet are one and the same. The general consensus is that she must grab the wrong box of chocolate squares when she makes her fudge frosting because for days after consumption, there is a definite beaten path to the bathrooms of every Flomdahl relative who dared feast on the chocolate wonders.

There was an additional tray of cold cuts this year that Uncle Albert and Uncle Henry brought over. It was quite a selection. I don't know how those two bachelors manage that big old farmstead by themselves. It sounds as if maybe Aunt Gracie might move in with them now that Uncle Frank has passed on. (You knew about that didn't you? Something about a pig pen rumble.) Anyway, that should help out a little. I hope she can get past the cluttered hallway when she goes over there. I heard there are newspapers from the Hindenburg disaster still piled next to the door. And get this. Both uncles still had on long underwear at the reunion. I could see the ribbed cuffs hanging over their boots and peaking out from the wrists of their plaid flannel shirts. It was 87 degrees outside! Guess maybe those union suits are part of their skin by now.

During the non-ending table conversation someone asked the uncles how their well-seasoned team of horses was doing. Those two would have to be at least twenty-five years old by now...the horses, that is. How old do you think Uncle Albert and Uncle Henry are? I thought they were a hundred and ten when we used to visit the farm as kids. Remember how we would ask all the time if we could take a ride on Maude and Pearl? Then when the uncles finally relented and put us on their swayed backs (the horses, that is) we bawled our heads off until they lifted us down? From our point of view those horses seemed to be over fifty feet high. The chickens looked like ants from that height, remember? (Do you think it might actually have been ants we were seeing?)

Anyway, back to the cold cuts. As I mentioned before, someone, maybe it was me, it's just kind of a blur right now, asked Uncle Albert and Uncle Henry how Maude and Pearl were coming along. Without missing a beat and showing no facial expression whatsoever, (I'm sure you are picturing this right now from memory, which is all you have since you no longer come to the reunions, thanks to Fluff

Fluff), Uncle Albert's words just came thrusting forward with no emphasis anywhere for impression. In just one ambling, monotone trail, he laid it out to all who sat before him.

"Ahh, folks," he said most sadly, "I'm afraid old Pearl took to feeling pretty poorly last week and we had to call the ol' doc out and have 'er put down. A pity it was. Just a pity. Now you all just enjoy those cold cuts. They're pretty special."

I saw twenty hands swipe a clean path across twenty plates as cold cuts went sliding down the lace edging of the table linen. You just knew each and every Flomdahl was waiting on his or her turn for that most welcome visit from old Ralph.

All in unison, those thinly sliced delicacies disappeared... all, that is, except for the ones heaped up on Aunt Tillie's plate, who apparently did not, as I had formerly suspected, get a hearing aid since our last get-together. She gave no hint that she had heard the latest equine news report. She asked for seconds from the deli plate! Do you think Pearl was a guest at the table? Ooooh, I can't think about it. It looked like good old farm-raised beef to me. I'd attest to that, but then I'm no expert on protein cuts. Say, do you remember Bessie? I wonder if she's still in that wooden pen at the back of the uncles' barn. Or... do you suppose...? Pearl? Bessie? Don't let me go there. After all those years of service, they don't deserve to end up on a plate.

Well, dear cousin. I hope you can see now from my short note to you (well, not so short, I guess) all that you missed by not being at the latest gathering of the Flomdahl congregation. You know, Cousin, it would be a most generous move on your part if you were to lock up Fluff Fluff in the closet or chain him to your leg for a week or two before next year's reunion (it's the second Sunday in July as you well know...the same weekend Fluff Fluff meets his yearly Maker) to avoid any further life-stealing accident occurring to that invincible cat of yours. Then you could come and enjoy all the goodies with the rest of the Flomdahl clan. I feel guilty taking second helpings when I'd be more than happy to share the extras with you. Maybe with a little encouragement we can even get Aunt Florence to bring some of those saliva-curdling, hair-straightening homemade dill pickles of hers to the feast. Wouldn't it be worth a trip out to the country place just to see Ralph's reaction to those? Hope to see you next summer at the farm.

Your favorite cousin,

Victoria

P.S. On second thought, I might not make it to the reunion next year after all. I just bought a cat.

July 10

Dear Cousin T. R. (Oh, whoops, I mean Theodora),

(I still want to call you T. R. the way I did when we were growing up. What does the "R" stand for anyway? I guess I never did know your middle name.)

Just a short note to tell you we were all thinking of you this past weekend at the reunion and admiring you for staying back another year to tend to your parents. How are they feeling now? Have you found out the cause of their stiff necks and the pulled muscles in their backs? I stopped by to visit them a couple weeks ago and they seemed quite well. I was a little concerned when I first arrived and rang the doorbell. No one came to the door for several minutes. I could hear the polka music on the radio so I was pretty certain they were home. I was just about to go around to the back door when your dad came out to the porch and let me in.

As I walked into the living room I saw your mother trying to lower the Venetian blind that covers that window facing the parsonage. I don't think it has been lowered for some time because after she pulled the string it hung lopsided and would only go down on the right side about 6 inches from the top metal frame. I walked over with intentions of trying to fix it for her but she came toward me in a rush and said she would deal with it later. I did take a quick glance at the pull string and noticed that there was a clothespin clamped about 6 inches down from the top.

As we all walked to the sitting area I remember now that I saw your mother rubbing her neck and your father seemed to be massaging his shoulders, so perhaps this infirmity has been settling in for some time. Also I should maybe mention that I noticed their attention span seemed to be quite short. Or I guess I would say they were easily distracted.

Every time a car drove past on the road in front of their house both of your parents ran to the window. I made a point of carrying on a meaningful conversation to see if they could stay focused. I asked questions about several of their neighbors to which they responded in kind as to what most of them had been up to lately. But I couldn't help but notice how much more information they seemed to glean with great detail the happenings that took place at the next-door parsonage. They seemed quite informed and most eager to tell me about the goings-on in that big white house.

The first thing they told me was that they had "heard" that the new young minister, Reverend Burtness, would often step out in the early morning light to retrieve the morning paper wearing only his blue pajama bottoms and that one morning "someone" had heard a giggle and that Mrs. Reverend Burtness had tiptoed up behind the clergyman wearing only a blue long-sleeved pajama top! ("Scandalous" sleepwear I believe they called it…your mother did anyway. Your dad's eyes seemed to brighten at the mention of it). As the good Reverend had leaned over to pick up the paper, the reverend's young wife (they had only been married about six months) had reached out to pull at the elastic waist of her husband's pajamas, but nobody saw anything they shouldn't see (and here I noticed that both of your parents looked somewhat disappointed) because just as the elastic was stretched outward, with a promise of going downward (?), Voegel's milk delivery truck went by. The noise had distracted both the on-lookers and the early-awakened young couple.

The newlyweds quickly darted back toward the house, laughing as they ran barefooted over the driveway. Stopping at the door before opening it, the muscular reverend (your mother gave out a huge sigh while giving this description, earning her a dark, rankled look from your father. I believe he missed hearing her say the word Adonis, or who knows what his reaction might have been) anyway, this was when the virile religious leader (my added trait for him since I now was picturing him in my own mind) handed the rolled up newspaper to his blushing bride and then reaching out had lifted her into his arms. As he gave her a most passionate kiss, the morning headlines fell to the ground and there was no doubt that there would be a delay in finding out the latest news.

Both of your parents sighed in remembrance of the moment and were decidedly distracted as the image returned to circle around in their minds. I cleared my throat loudly to remind them they had a visitor still in their midst.

I didn't ask them any more questions about the young church leaders from next door, but your parents continued to offer tidbits about things that took place there every day. They seemed to think that the good Reverend must not be able to stay at the church across the street too long without taking a coffee break. His daily routine was to leave for the office about 8:00 A.M., return to the parsonage at 9:30, no doubt for a few cups of the caffeine-laced drink; back to the office at 10:00, another twenty minute break around 11:00 and then it was time for lunch shortly after that. A similar schedule of timed intervals continued each afternoon. Your parents surmised that the young minister didn't know that too much caffeine could increase your anxiety level. Besides, they noticed that his face was always flushed a deep scarlet when he came out of the house causing them to wonder if the coffee was already giving him a reaction.

Well, anyway, I decided I now was more acquainted with the young couple than I needed to be, so I told your parents I really should be on my way. They were starting to walk me to the door, when a screen door slammed next door and they both took off for the window where the Venetian blind was hanging at its precarious angle. I looked up as I heard the cuckoo clock next to the window sound off eleven times. It was my guess that that the "caffeine addict" was returning for replenishment.

I said good-bye as I went to let myself out. I turned back toward your parents one more time before making my exit and saw both of them trying to solicit a farewell wave. I heard grunting and moaning as they tried to convince their muscles that it could be done. They didn't succeed.

I do hope that Aunt Irene and Uncle Ted are soon back to their normal selves. Aunt Josie said they asked you to move their sleeper couch over next to the window…so they could catch the warm rays of sun as they lay recovering. She also said they ordered a bigger window for that side of the house and that it's being installed this week. They felt there just wasn't enough sun coming through those small panes.

We all admire you for taking such good care of your parents and hope we can see all of you one of these days soon. If there is anything you need or we can fill in for you when you need a break, please don't hesitate to call any of us. I understand many of the relatives have already offered to help, but you told them you hated to intrude on their time and really, you didn't mind at all. After all, you said, it's a daughter's privilege to help her parents in their time of need. You're really something. You know that? Keep in touch.

Your cousin,

V.J.
(By the way, *my* middle name is Jean)

P.S. I was cleaning out my closet the other day and found an old pair of binoculars. For some reason I thought of your parents. I don't know why I did that.

Be sure to greet them for me. Oh, I almost forgot.

Aunt Josie mentioned that you were starting to have problems with *your* neck, too. I certainly hope you can find out what's causing that seemingly contagious ailment and get it healed. We'd love to see all three of you at the reunion one of these years. If you should see Reverend Burtness and his pretty little wife, say hello to them for me. I've never met them, but somehow I feel as if I know them intimately.

July 11

Dear Cousin Shirleen,

I just want to send you a short note about the reunion this past weekend and to say I was so sorry to hear that you had another operation this year. It just isn't the same when you're not there. Of course, as always, you had a good reason for missing it. If I'm not mistaken the last time you were there you brought your new red and green jump rope I think you had just gotten it as a present for your 8th birthday and you, Cousin Loretta and I played that one game you made up. How did it go? "Squash that beetle. Squish that bug. Sweep their bloody innards right under the rug!" Or something like that. You were always so good with words. If you aren't a writer you should give it some thought.

You've missed a lot of reunions, haven't you. Aunt Josie said she had planned to come stay with you for a couple days last week after your surgery so she could keep you supplied with Jello until your throat healed but that you had told her you thought you could handle the recovery days alone this year. Mothers just never quit being mothers, do they. After dinner on Sunday I noticed there was some of that good Jello with the fruit cocktail in it left over so I mentioned to Aunt Josie that you might enjoy something with a little substance to it after having had liquids most of last week. She said that I was just waaay too thoughtful and was so pleased at the suggestion that she left with the extra bowlful before the dishes were even done. On her way out the door I saw her wrap a couple of Aunt Serena's brownies in a napkin and slip them into her purse. I have tried calling her the past two days, but she must not be close to the phone. I hope you enjoyed the Jello. You don't have to thank me. I was happy to do it for you.

After your mother told me about your tonsillectomy, I got to thinking that you must be some sort of medical wonder. Isn't this the seventh time those tonsils have grown back? It seems to me that was what kept you away from the Flomdahl bash last year…and the year before that and the year… Well, I just couldn't get it out of my mind that this was really a rarity and I decided that if you had to suffer through so many operations, you should get some notoriety out of it. So I want to inform you that you will probably be getting a verification form by mail within the next week or so from the publicity offices of The Guinness Book of World Records. I can't imagine that anyone has had tonsils grow back more times than you have. Let me know when you hear from the publishers. It would be so exciting to see a Flomdahl make it into that famous book of records.

Well, I guess I should close for now. I have a couple other notes to write yet today. Have you seen Cousin Robert lately? He didn't make it to the reunion either this weekend. I guess the day before the reunion someone told his little Billy that there was no Santa Claus and surprise, surprise, no Easter Bunny either and that all those gifts come from his mom and dad. From what Aunt Florence said, her grandson was so mad at his dad, now that he knows he's the one who buys the gifts, that he locked himself in his room and wasn't coming out until he got the riding pony he asked for last Christmas. Billy apparently wasn't buying the excuse any longer that Santa couldn't carry a horse along in his sleigh when he was flying all around the world.

I wonder if Cousin Robert remembers the one Christmas Eve so many years ago that he leaned over and whispered into one little girl's ear that all that Santa Claus stuff was a lot of bunk and, as if that wasn't enough to shatter a trunk full of childhood dreams, he also delivered a further blow by saying that in this great world of "Let's Pretend," you couldn't possibly find a rabbit anywhere on this earth who would be able to carry a whole basketful of colored eggs and marshmallow candy around his furry little neck even if he tried! Such a heartbreaking revelation. One never forgets the person who destroyed one's youthful fantasies.

It was so nice seeing Billy at the playground on Saturday. I was out for my morning walk and just happened to see him on the swings. We had a short visit. He's really growing.

I do hope you are feeling better and are back to eating solid foods. Were you able to chew the fruit cocktail? Your mother said she would bring you more when you finished that bowlful. I mentioned to her that it was your favorite treat and that you wished she would bring it more often.

Your sympathetic cousin,

Vicky

P.S. Be sure to let me know when you hear from the Guinness people. I guess they like to double-check all entries to verify that everything is on the "up-and-up" before adding a record to their prestigious book. I imagine some people make things up for one reason or another. It will be nice seeing you at the reunion next July.

July 11

Dear Cousin Robert,

I've been thinking of you so much the past few days and thought I would write just a short note to let you know you have been on my mind. I certainly hope all is well at your house. From what Aunt Florence told us at the reunion on Sunday you had a little problem this weekend with Billy. The poor thing. He did finally unlock the bedroom door, didn't he? Isn't there just always someone around to poke a hole in a balloon of dreams? He'll probably get over it soon, although sometimes it can take years and years to recover from a shock such as that. I mean, the joy one feels as a child as he (or as the case may be…she) listens for the sleigh bells as they hover over the rooftop (I know I always heard them until a certain someone…) And then the revelation that the Easter Bunny doesn't stay up all night coloring eggs and hiding them… Well, as I said, it can be quite a jolt to such a tender little system.

We missed not having you at the Flomdahl reunion this past Sunday. You haven't been there for quite a few years, have you? I've been trying to think of the reason you weren't there last year. Oh, yes, now I remember. Aunt Florence had said you called her and mentioned that Billy had had a bad reaction after eating a chocolate sundae or something that had chocolate in it. Those chocolate allergies can be quite serious, I'm told. Are you supervising him carefully? Because if I'm not mistaken the year before that you couldn't make it to the family farmstead either because Billy had broken out in a rash from eating a Hershey bar. (Aunt Florence couldn't remember the reason for THAT absence, but I haven't forgotten). And wasn't there another get-together that you told your mother you couldn't attend because your allergy prone son had eaten a cookie with chocolate chips in it? Bobby, you really should watch that boy more closely.

Well, I guess I should get busy here. I just wanted to let you know we missed you on Sunday. Oh, by the way, did Billy mention that I saw him at the park on Saturday? He was playing on the swings and he said that after a few more times back and forth he was going to make a trip to the grocery store and get some Ding Dongs…those "chocolate" cream-filled cakes with the thick fudge frosting. You know which ones I mean, don't you? He said every Saturday you give him money so he can buy them. It's his favorite treat. I thought that strange because of his allergy problem and told him I thought he really shouldn't eat them if he always broke out in a rash from chocolate. He wrinkled up his face and wanted to know where I'd heard that. Said he's never had a rash in his life and what was a rash, anyway? He said he ate chocolate every day. I had a few more words with him...just a "casual" conversation...and then I guess he must have changed his mind about going to the store because instead of heading toward town he took off down the sidewalk yelling your name and something about a "stupid sleigh" and a "basketful of eggs." It looked as if he was heading straight home. Hope this finds you all well.

Your cousin,

Vick

P.S. Do you know I'm the only cousin who's ever at all the reunions? I hope you'll be able to make it to the next one. Gramps mentioned something about revising his will next summer. Should I save you a place by me at the table?

July 13

Dear Gram and Gramps,

I'm sending you just a short note to thank you for the delightful time I had on Sunday. It's always so great to see everyone again, smell the tantalizing odors that surround that huge old dining room table, sample the familiar goodies and give our taste buds a surprise with some of the new treats.

We're lucky to know that everyone cares about all the good times we have but also to be able to share the difficult times with each other and know we will get the support we need to meet with those trying times. I told everyone at the dinner that it would be a really nice gesture if each of them would send a sympathy card or "thinking of you" note to Cousin Loretta since the tragedy with her cat was so sad. I passed her address around to all the relatives. I also gave out Cousin Shirleen's address so they could send her a get-well card. That girl has certainly suffered with throat problems. And I hope you didn't mind that I took up a collection for Billy. I'll send the money to him and tell him to put it toward the saddle his dad will have to buy for that pony he's getting this week. That should make Billy forget about his awful rash. Oh, and one more thing. As I drove down the street past Uncle Ted's and Aunt Irene's place this morning, all their windows were bare. Apparently they were letting in every ray of healing sunshine that is available. I hope they feel well soon. As I looked across the street from their house, I noticed the display case in front of the Lutheran church where that young minister serves. I'm sure Uncle Ted has told you about him and his pretty little wife. Anyway, the theme for next week's sermon was already printed in bold black letters on the front of the case. The title instructs to all: "Observe Thy Neighbor and Know His Ways." I wonder if Uncle Ted and Aunt Irene will feel well enough to attend. But then, they already seem like the kind who would be very attentive to their neighbors. I think they have also instilled that worthy trait into Cousin Theodora. They are all such caring people and always seem to spend more time in concern for others than for themselves.

Say, Gram and Gramps, I'm not sure if you two believe in that psychic stuff or not, but I seem to be getting a mental message that we're going to have a much bigger crowd at the reunion next year. I can't explain it. It's just a feeling I have. Come next July, Gram, I think you're finally going to get to use your whole set of Melmac dishes. That big old farm table is going to look like a summer garden when it's set with all those plates splashed with orange, yellow, and blue posies with cups to match. And those green plaid napkins are going to add just the finishing touch.

I just want to thank both of you once more for all the happy Flomdahl memories you have given the rest of us all these years. You two are the dearest example of abiding love and devoted caring that this world could ever know. You're a hard act to follow. Take care of each other; stay happy and healthy. Let me know if you need any groceries before Thursday, otherwise I'll pick up your list then. Love you much.

Your granddaughter,

Victoria Jean

P.S. Give Ralph a hug from me, would you?
He's such a special addition to our reunions.
Even when we can't see him, somehow we just
know he is there. I don't know what we'd ever do
without him.

****

virginia rasmussen

About The Author

Virginia Rasmussen is a published poet and author whose first book *Calico Days and Sandpaper Knights* reviewed the lives of two elderly widows and the thoughts, dreams, and heartache that made up their album of lifetime memories.

While Virginia's storylines portray heartfelt circumstances that can affect people of all ages, she also counterbalances the serious tones with lighter, more carefree moments. They may not always be the "laugh out loud" types of humor, but the "tongue in cheek" responses can also be refreshing and uplifting.

Virginia and her husband, Jay, who were born and raised in southern Minnesota, now live in a log cabin surrounded by the north woods of Wisconsin. They are the parents of four grown children.

Printed in the United States
746700001B